PIG COOKIES AND OTHER STORIES

"This is what he said to her with the mouth of his eyes, before he could get close enough to use breath: he was coming here today to tell her, here was the beginning of their story."

—from "Sawyers Along the River"

Set earlier this century in a small village in northern Mexico, these interrelated stories revolve around extraordinary characters whose fortunes rise and fall in the eyes of their ever-watchful neighbors.

Among the many memorable townspeople is Lázaro Luna, whose life is the most interwoven with others. He'll later become mayor ("Five") and a surrogate husband ("A Trick on the World"), but we meet him in the title story as a young boy so much in love that his hands can't concentrate on the pig cookies he's baking. The result is a "batter of surprise" and the most popular cookies the village has ever eaten, each one a different shape, each telling a different story.

Don Lázaro and other endearing characters populate the lyrical and enchanting world of Alberto Alvaro Ríos, a place where "there is no need of wind, not with so many whispers."

PIG
COOKIES

Other books by Alberto Alvaro Ríos:

POETRY

Teodoro Luna's Two Kisses
The Lime Orchard Woman
Five Indiscretions
Whispering to Fool the Wind

FICTION

The Iguana Killer (Stories)

PIG
COOKIES

and other stories

Alberto Alvaro Ríos

CHRONICLE BOOKS
SAN FRANCISCO

Printed in the United States of America.

Library of Congress Cataloging-in-Publication Data:
Ríos, Alberto.
      Pig cookies and other stories / by Alberto Alvaro Ríos.
          p.   cm.
      ISBN 0-8118-0745-2 (pbk.)
      I. Title.
PS3568.I587P5   1995
813'.54—dc20   94-22103
                                                CIP

The author would like to thank the editors and early readers of this
manuscript for their abiding enthusiasm.

Some of the stories in this collection originally appeared in the following
magazines: "Champagne Regions" in *Willow Springs*; "Five" in *Colorado
Review*; "The Great Gardens of Lamberto Diaz" in *Gettysburg Review*;
"Mr. Todasbodas" as "All-Weddings" in *The Ohio Review*; "Not Like Us"
as "Triton Himself" in *The North American Review*; "Pig Cookies" in
Colorado Review; "Saturnino el Magnífico" in *Story*; "Sawyers Along the
River" in *Manoa*; "Spiced Plums" in *Sonora Review*; "Susto" in *Mid-
American Review*; "Trains at Night" in *Ploughshares*; "A Trick On the
World" as "Lázaro in Paris" in *Blue Mesa Review*; "Waltz of the Fat Man"
in *The Kenyon Review*.

Book and cover design: Gretchen Scoble
Composition: On Line Typography
Cover illustration: Gerald Bustamante

Distributed in Canada by Raincoast Books,
8680 Cambie Street, Vancouver, B.C. V6P 6M9

10 9 8 7 6 5 4 3 2 1

Chronicle Books
275 Fifth Street
San Francisco, CA 94103

For Joaquín Alvaro Jesús Ríos

Contents

I NEVER LIKED PIG COOKIES very much. But they were what you got growing up in the Fifties along the border—pig cookies at birthday parties, on Christmas, Saints' days, and the rest. Pig cookies were part of our child's litany of sweets, along with the light brown, near-liquid bars of fudge, the *cajeta,* and *ciruelas,* and those little plastic packets of colored, sugar-and-chili *tamarindo.* But because the gingerbread cookies looked like pigs, well, that was the thing. Who could resist them, lying fresh-made on a tray in the bakery.

And that's all it took: as a child, if you laughed, just once, at someone dangling a pig cookie in front of you, then the whole family from then on thought they were your favorite. Because of that, they've been around for centuries. Ask anyone.

Cochitos, they are called in Mexico, and people still say—"remember how you used to like *cochitos?*" But I never did. I liked the chewy *cajeta* much better, even if I didn't know what it was, exactly. I even liked the vague taste of the balsa wood box the *cajeta* came in, whose top you would have to break in half and then use as a spoon to get the stuff out.

But gingerbread is gingerbread. You might like other things better, all right. You might like them a lot better. But pig cookies—you don't forget pig cookies.

THE DAY MY FATHER was born, the volcano Tacaná erupted a few miles down from the house in which his family was living, a house with large windows in the tropics, at the southernmost tip of Mexico—Tapachula, on the border of Guatemala. My grandmother tells me what she most remembers from that day is how birds came into the house, how they tore the mosquito nettings. The birds, a great many tens of birds, came in and sat themselves up on the sapling rafters to escape the ash and mountain pieces. The noise they made became, in her mind, the noise my father made as he was being born.

They were living in Tapachula at that time because my grandfather, Margarito, was inextricably involved in the Mexican Revolution, and he kept his family at the edges of the Republic—in the northern Nogales and the southern Tapachula—so that, in case his side lost, the family might take one more step quickly into another land.

The boat in which my father's family had sailed to Tapachula from a point higher up on the coast sank the day they got there; my grandmother tells me how, floating in the bay, she was rescued, and how as she floated all she could hear were the three band members on the boat playing the only thing they could think of, "Más cerca mi dios a ti," and then how she could not hear them, only people crying and chickens.

The boat they came on had sunk; the boat they would take to leave would not come. But it was not just my grandmother there waiting for her husband to come home happy or dead. The side stories of revolution were there in Tapachula, a whole town of displaced people put on hold, taken out of time, not so different from the Nogales in which I was raised, and where the rest of the family was waiting. Nogales was on the opposite side of Mexico, on the border with Arizona.

Nogales and Tapachula were, for my family, both the same town. They were towns next to countries, but inside countries as well.

This was the border, what we called "the line." It is not, finally, an external, physical line, as maps and the border patrol and immigration would have. The line is, more cleverly, inside, where jeeps cannot go. This is the true line.

THE DAY MY FATHER was born, the president of Mexico at the moment, Alvaro Obregón, on whose side my grandfather Margarito had been fighting, was to come to Tapachula and christen my father, who had been named in his honor, Alvaro Alberto. He would have come because Don Margarito was his right hand, in place of the one Obregón had literally lost in an earlier campaign. He would have come, but was assassinated. The future for my father, for his family, for that town, at that moment was unimaginable. 1928–29. The Thirties.

The volcano Tacaná had erupted in the state of Chiapas, near Tapachula. The stock market in the north would crash. Hitler's war would come to Mexico in boats. Augusto César Sandino had taken hold to the south, his Sandinistas fighting U.S. Marines. He would be assassinated by the first Somoza. Leon Trotsky, banished from Russia, would come here to be assassinated, and the schoolchildren — my father — would learn the "Internationale" so that he might be remembered. Pancho Villa, Alvaro Obregón, Venustiano Carranza, each a side of the revolution, had all been assassinated. Artaud would come here and catch the theater of cruelty in his head, and Breton, and all the others, everyone from the edge. It was a mutual attraction. Everything was nothing; there was nowhere else to go, but one could not stay here.

THIS IS ALL MINE, what I inherit, even the name, but backward, Alberto Alvaro, because everything was turned around, and the name had to come out that way. I was born of people who were outside of time and place, people who were displaced and unsure, people reduced ultimately to manners rather than to laws for survival. They found the line inside themselves, the things they would and would not do, in there. Their lives are from before the border fences.

This was my family—Margarito, Refugio, Clemente, Ventura, and all of them—a people between wars, between cultures, between governments. They didn't need a fence to tell them this. The churches in Mexico had been closed down but did not disappear; the Chinese had been deported, but had not gone. The Depression and the stock market crash had happened in the United States, but now the United States was everywhere, and what happened there happened to everyone. The border finally was not a fence. It was the decade itself.

If there was uncertainty in those years, there was also its opposite. It was the law of physics. The everyday was still the everyday; a headache was still a headache, and a pig cookie, well. These were the constants from the realm of certainty. The seasons, the circus, a good dinner at the finish of a day. This was the gingerbread of living. In the years when the circus came, everything seemed possible, as anyone could see that walking the high wire had little to do with the confines of a canvas tent. If the people were uncertain, the performers were bold. If there was, in sum, general disaffection in this world and in this place, there could also be found a wild love for two clowns, for an elephant and a couple of horses.

PIG
COOKIES

Saturnino el Magnífico

THE ENTIRE CIRCUS TRAIN fell in the manner of a child's toy into the ravine just outside of town, its cars folding up in the fall so that from a distance they looked like the rough-angled line of teeth on a saw. The regular engineers from the federal railroad all knew the bank of the wide turn, and gave their trains some speed, but the circus came to this place only once every four years, and their engineer this time was new.

Moving out of town, the train came to such a point of angle, such a crookedness, the floor no longer a floor, that everyone and everything on the train moved or was moved to the left side to look. And when they did look, they saw themselves, falling into the dirt and the dark, falling and being jerked, so that their shouts did not go forward from their mouths, were not fast enough. For the length of the moment it seemed their voices came from the backs of their heads.

The circus train crashed a crash of spectacle, which, everyone later agreed, so showed the honesty of these performers that the townspeople felt better about having attended and paid good money for what had seemed a suspect affair the night before, even though they had enjoyed themselves.

THE ELEPHANT SATURNINO only half stood, or was only half fallen, at half-height on his knees when the two boys saw him.

They looked at him and said, it cannot be. The great elephant in this moment was a little boy himself, again kneeling at a game of marbles, reaching as if he were a cheater with his great arm into the game's circle.

Or else with his trunk the elephant in comic pantomime was making fun of the caboose man's arm as he had made desperate signs to the engineer just a few minutes ago, that arm shaking to be understood, furious in its shake, furious at the failing of words in whose stead this shaking arm now found itself.

The elephant Saturnino looked half as tall as the truth, and helpless even with all his strength on the painful knees of his unsure legs, his capacious trunk moving back and around.

And then his trunk did begin to talk, that caboose man's flailing arm, with what looked like a mouth stolen from a man's face on its end. The elephant Saturnino's trunk began making all the noise it had made from all the years of his life all at once, the noise a drowning man's arm would make if it had the voice.

The scene evoked the picture of a performing trombonist, of a vacuum cleaner hose gone wild, in that particular depiction of action which cartoons in theaters all use sooner or later. But this was a mighty hose, upon which no storybook face would have been convincing.

That this scene was further filled with the rest of the circus train and the rest of the animals and the rest of the clowns and tightrope walkers and fire-eaters, revved an engine of color and noise and excitement more than equal to the best moments of this circus's long history.

This was the wreck of a circus train. This was what the sad boy Tavito Cano, who had been by chance walking along the tracks at this very moment, came into town yelling about, happy almost to bring news this big. It filled him so much he thought he had grown.

Animals, loose feathers, smoke, humidity, night and small fires, a noise from the insides of things, from the insides of bright oranges and yellows, a moan from the purple that would not stop, a red all pain, all noise but not for ears.

In trying to get someone to come to the train's wreck, Tavito Cano's loud yelling and gestures could not properly give over to the townspeople gathered the true spectrum of occurrence. He could not adequately compare it to anything anyone here had seen, so many whirrings of wheels still, so many of the smallest pieces of universe still in the air, so that they almost did not believe him.

JOSÉ AND LÁZARO RAN quickly to the train, understanding something about the gravity of Tavito's words more quickly than the rest because they were boys as well.

"Quickly, a hand!"

The circus man with the long moustaches, moustaches which were themselves advertisement for his place in the world, moustaches which were themselves arms so folded as to flex muscles of their own—this circus man called to the two boys. Or at least they thought he was calling to them, so loud were his words and so much did they fit into the ears of these two boys, eager.

He was the man, after all, who with his real arms only just last night had held thousands of pounds of iron and stone and flesh. He was the man who had held three women borrowed from the trapeze acts on each of his arms, with a seventh in high heeled shoes standing with her back to the audience, her heels on his brows and the balls of her feet on his skull in that way he said he did not mind.

"A hand!"

Who would have thought that he could not by himself control the simpleness of a single wild elephant, could not grab a hold of that trunk, whirl the elephant into a dizzied spin and stupor, then rubbing his hands together finish his natural business of saving the day.

The boys had thought the advertising posters for the circus to have said as much, and so they hesitated at his call. It smacked of the way in which some performers call for volunteers from the audience and then hypnotize them into biting off their own arms, the way they had heard, the way José said his mother had said that his one-armed uncle had been so foolish.

"You there!" he called again, and with greater urgency.

José and Lázaro looked at each other and shrugged their shoulders. They started in his direction, but could not get over the fact of their having to help, so experienced were they now as dazzled members of the audience from the night before, as dazzled members of the audience who had given themselves over to this man, who had taken such good care of them. How could it be that he was asking for their help: this is what the shrugging of their shoulders said.

"Over here, quickly," he said, gesturing to the right with the full egg of his head.

But then again, of course he would call on them. Had they not believed this all their short lives? That, as this man was superhuman, so were they also superhuman, that this was the proper and clear domain of two boys in a wild world: to be masters of everything, to have under their clothes their own large initials in red, that law of membership in the world of champions they had learned well from the comic books.

If he were not in fact singling them out with his words and the movements of his hands, they nonetheless believed themselves, at that moment, unquestionably chosen.

He could have called on any of the others in the crowd, on the men who had all come right behind the two boys. But José and Lázaro knew what was what. They recognized the call to action—*at last*—as heroes on behalf of the Forces of Good In This World.

These boys threw themselves into the task of helping him untangle and calm the elephant Saturnino, but not without saying to each other with their eyes that this might still be some trick, some even more breathtaking part of the singular performance from the evening previous still lingering. It had cost enough money, after all, so that to think of this as still part of the show was not beyond the limits of the already-prodded imagination.

JOSÉ AND LÁZARO COULD not have been more in agreement that the elephant Saturnino el Magnífico had won this battle of wills between himself and the strongman, whose true name was given by the owner of the circus as Don Noé, but whose last name he would say to no one, only that he was a black sheep in this world.

The elephant would not bow his great head on command, which was certainly an occasion for sadness, inasmuch as from the battle the strongman would not be returning. This was what happened to strongmen, the boys later said. Nobody after all ever sees an old one.

Through what seemed to the boys as hours of struggle with the beast, this Don Noé did more than his share, as was his way. But the elephant had its memory, the way they say elephants do not forget, which also presumably means they do not, as well, forgive.

With that memory it remembered whatever there was to remember about all of its years with the circus. The involuntary performances done as a favor to this man. The silly hats and the cumbersome saddle. The cartwheels and the anthem-singing, and the clean-up afterward, the rolling of circus tent-poles onto the train, the lifting of steamer trunks into the hoisted nettings of the docks.

The work, and the work again, and for not much, almost nothing, since an elephant after the show in the company of performers is so big no one sees it—this elephant, angry for so many years, angry and with wounds, finally took from this Don Noé more than his life. A life, after all, is simple. But a friendship at a moment of anger, this is something else, something more.

The final manner in which the struggle was lost for control of the elephant was not something repeatable in conversation, and in the face of what the elephant did next, José and Lázaro had to stand back. Their small arms and puny pushes had effected no purchase of the grand master bull elephant's soul.

They had been no help, this much was clear. For a moment the two boys looked at each other, and saw only two boys and nothing more. Perhaps he had been calling to the men after all. But the men had seen they could make no difference, and so no man had stepped forward.

In that night's extraordinary moment the elephant Saturnino el Magnífico took the life both from Don Noé's body and from the memories of the boys. They did not want to remember. They were told not to. They could not: something so big did not fit onto a place so small as their tongues. There were no words.

Like the caboose man and like Saturnino himself, there were no words for Don Noé at the very end, and so he took a bow. That was all, but it was everything against which words must always fail.

That he took a bow in thanks at the end of his life, that he took a bow at the singular moment before everything happened, this was too big for José and Lázaro to hold inside.

But it was not the bow itself. Instead, it was the risk of such an act that mattered. It was not a risk in that there was danger; rather, the risk was in what people would think, and then say, in response to a true moment of simple and profound grace.

That was the risk finally: to give away something of the self, and hope that people would take it away with them, a little for each but plenty to go around.

Noé's was a most composed and methodical gesture of body at the end. His bones moved into position with a slowness and a balance, a perfect weariness, something in which his body was practiced.

At that moment, the circus was, after all, the most remarkable entertainment of the near-middle of the twentieth century, and he was, as promised, its star, whose fame would outlive the moon itself.

THE BAD JOKE OF this all, of course, Lázaro would think later, is that, while the circus muscleman kept yelling for the two boys to give him a hand, finally it was his very own hand they saw as it flew through the air, not trapeze-like at all. They saw it taken from the stem of his arm and thrown like a rose flower to the floor of the bull-ring by what seemed to be the lady's hand of the elephant's trunk, that pink thing part inside of the gray glove.

Lázaro would remember how then it was as if the whole roar of the crowd, perhaps the roars of all the crowds Don Noé had ever heard through his ears, upon having his hand taken from him, suddenly came out through his mouth, as a scream.

That it was a hand and not an arm, this was the gesture of friendship, the terrible delicacy, the small detail conveyed in a whisper late at night when everyone else has gone home. A hand and not an arm. Only a friend takes that much.

At first, Lázaro would think, the sound had seemed borrowed, as if Noé had not himself ever had need of such a sound. But then it filled out, and became his to the end.

THAT NIGHT AND THE next day after the accident, there was of course an investigation.

Don Noé The Black Sheep, the owner called him, having heard it of someone who had once claimed to be a member of Noé's family. His people had lived for the most part farther north than the small towns in the jungles where the circus had traveled.

Neither would the owner give the last name of this Don Noé The Black Sheep, even after he died a little later from the bleeding, still in the arm of his elephant, who was sorry, and who wanted to help him—his only recourse being to keep everyone else away, to still be a wild and monstrous beast all around, but not at its center, not where it held Don Noé. It was wrong, but it was all the elephant could do, hold the man who had held him.

It was wrong for Don Noé because nobody could save him, and it was wrong for the elephant, who soon enough, because he would no longer eat, and no longer lift himself in song, shrank to the size of a large, hunched rabbit. It was wrong, but it was all he could do.

For some months, the new managers of the circus showed the elephant off that way, as much a marvel in this body as he was in the other.

But Saturnino died too, or rather, more disappeared than died, worn down like a stain on pants that at first seems like such a tragedy but which through use and washings begins to go away.

THE ACTUAL NIGHT OF the billed circus performance had been an affair of Byzantine triangles, between humans, between animals, sometimes with machines, and with glitter dust. There had been the obligatory wondrous throwing of impossible numbers of objects and children through the air. All the performers' hands in the air moved fast. White-gloved in the bad lighting, their hands seemed to make the bright lines of a tree branch ignited in a campfire and waved quickly through the air.

One expected the hands with their trailing lights to spell something, and they did, from childhood, from the practicing of penmanship, the many-O line, the O over and over, until the O took flight up into the stands, up into the crowds, onto the line of their mouths.

It was as if the hands of these performers were so fast in their movement that the movement itself was something of substance, so that with the flick of the wrist one of the white-faced harlequins spun an O out like a gentle bullet, like a moth, into the mouths of the audience.

And the O took hold, like sugar from a doughnut, and followed into the throat, and therein lay the source of the sound of the room, so many O's, as if someone finally read all the lines from the penmanship books, read them as if they were lines from a play, OOOO. It was the audience's part in the script, and the job was done well.

The night of the scheduled performance and the night subsequent—these were both the circus. Every night was a performance, billed or not. The circus was the circus without fail, without rest, always ready to put on a show, always fresh from the inhuman jungles of Chiapas and Tabasco, fresh from farther south still.

The death of the elephant, therefore, was taken into account. After the erasure of Saturnino el Magnífico, the rest of the circus performers took on part of the work of his elephant's great back, some keepsake of his absolute pleasure and displeasure, and became *EL CIRCO MAGNÍFICO* whose very name made noise on the page.

They later added as a subtitle, EL ESPECTÁCULO DE LOS SIGLOS, The Spectacle of the Centuries, and later, NO DISCOUNTS, but they had it right the first time.

This was the circus, and for the old strongman Don Noé there was a new strongman, who did not yet have even a first name. But a strongman is a strongman, and soon, so as to fill in the need for a name, people began to refer to this new man again as Don Noé, as if it were more than a name for a man. As if it were a name for the job as well. A level of rank. First the people called him in this way, and then the other performers.

Don Noé was not, after all, there to object. He had never been there to do anything but lift and move slowly, to heave and to groan. To be at one with the object he was moving, almost as if it were instead moving him. And here he was, his sounds sorted out once more. Here he was, young and true again.

In later years Lázaro lost track of his friend José, who was with him that night. But if he did not lose Don Noé, neither did he lose his friend José. Nobody gets lost finally, he thought. And Lázaro would find him, by walking backward in his sleep to that place. Lázaro liked José that way, a boy with the circus in town. It was a way to look at himself. They are always good friends there.

There, there was popcorn and peanuts, and fried plantains rolled in sugar, and *churros,* always something local, plum ices and God's-beard. These things, and sadness.

A WHOLE LINE OF PEOPLE came along the path to where the train had derailed. A whole line of people who had gathered to watch this man the night before stood in front of him once again. The men of the town tried to help, but there was no opening. José and Lázaro had gotten there first, and they were doing what could be done.

The men standing were carpenters and sweepers, a banker, the twins who owned the clothing shop. No Tarzan leapt from beneath their clothes, no surprise man in loincloth and leopard-skin. There was nothing hiding all these years in the soul of a townsman, nothing that could sweep José and Lázaro away and take care of this business as if it were something simply bothersome, a nuisance of time.

And for the women as well there was no place. No mother of a mad bull elephant who knew its language, no baker of a day's ingredients who could have made this, and so also know its possible remedy, its soothing tea of mint for the stomach or mustard plaster for the dull fish-hooks of the raspy voice and the drowned chest.

Nor for those in between, who were something of a man and a woman both, and a child and a beast: those who were the capillaries of this town like all towns, those who allowed for the real and smooth interchange of words between the sexes, those who, as with the dances and sugar in coffee, had brought the circus in the first place.

Lázaro would remember being told later that no one had liked the black sheep Don Noé very much, who was rumored never to have slept since his arrival, not even at night. Don Noé, who almost never raised his eyes, as if that act in his life were the most difficult feat of all.

That was all the more a bargain, Lázaro later thought. Knowing they would get to go home, and that the stakes this night would be high, but not too high because they did not like him very much: Pure, simple, this life-to-death moment of Noé's wrestling with the Magnífico was a show, and everyone once again was in his audience, thrilled to the edge of disbelief, without harness.

Pig Cookies

THIS WAS LÁZARO'S PLACE in the Luna family. His job, as far as anyone could remember, had always been to look up, then to turn red, to be on fire from shame about and from love for his brothers—both feelings at the same time. Why he felt shame for them as they spit or fought or made noises was easy enough to see, but why he loved them was more difficult. Some days, in moments that took his breath away, moments that were either fear or understanding or both, Lázaro thought he loved them for the same reasons they shamed him.

Nobody asked Lázaro to take the job of being responsible in public for his brothers. The job was his nonetheless, keeping the same hours as his eyes—when they were open, he was accountable for anything they took in. The transaction was simple. If Lázaro saw his brothers in the street do one thing or another, then there was no helping his face, which would simply catch fire before he could stop it.

Therein, he thought, lay the problem. Was he in fact a Luna? He did not, could not, act after all in the manner of his brothers. They took what they wanted and said what they thought. His brothers for example laughed and spat freely and regularly in the streets, in front of the whole town, without ever looking up to see who was watching. They did nothing illegal, not exactly. However, the things they did were not illegal only because no one had thought to make up laws for the simple politenesses of life.

This was what he was thinking that Tuesday morning when he said to himself, Lázaro, why don't you simply go and *ask* her.

He thought about his decision, and this was the problem. Lázaro had considered trying the manners of his brothers. But *asking,* this is not what a Luna man would do, he thought to himself, not what his brothers would do, not Teodoro, not Anselmo. The method of his family was simple, and always worked. They would go and *tell* her. It didn't matter about what. Their method was that simple.

But even as he thought of going and *telling* her she would be his wife, Lázaro knew with his stomach this would not work for him. *No,* thought Lázaro.

He was certainly as clever as his brothers. He could think up any number of ways to tell her, with force, with conviction, with the consent of her parents even. None of it would work, though—not if the head thought up these words instead of the stomach, where the true decisions are made.

Some people call this place of making decisions the heart. But Lázaro Luna thought to himself, again, *no.* It's the stomach, without question.

Lázaro was left, therefore, with finding a way of asking instead of telling her. This was his first time, and he could certainly ask no advice of his brothers. They were profoundly expert in their ways and so would not be able to further him in his deviance. His brothers were entirely without experience in asking for anything, and would only be able to throw up their hands in exasperation at him.

"Ass King," was all Teodoro his closest brother had said, the one time Lázaro had tried to talk this over at home. "King of the asses, ass king, you see what you are saying? Now stop it." Teodoro shook his head, which is where his answer had come from.

In some things, thought Lázaro, Teodoro was nonetheless correct. Lázaro could not go to her and *ask* if she knew how beautiful she was. He would be required at that moment to *tell* her, fully, and with force. It was like spitting, only nice, he thought.

Who knew how to do these things correctly, he said to himself with his shoulders in that shrug that speaks. Shoulders are like that sometimes. In the way that for him the stomach was the heart, so are the shoulders sometimes a man's mouth.

LÁZARO HAD MADE ARRANGEMENTS to meet her on the following Tuesday. Well, he thought, not *arrangements;* nothing in the plural, not so many chances. His was only one arrangement, one chance, perhaps his only chance to make the impression of a lifetime.

What he had made in fact was The Arrangement, the one. With the blessing of her parents, he was to meet her. The appointment would be in the parlor-lemonade-sit-down manner of these meetings. These first meetings have always been this way, for centuries. This was what he guessed.

Lázaro did not, after all, have any firsthand knowledge of what might happen, or even of what should happen. Still, he had only himself to ask. He would therefore have to imagine their meeting. Imagining was his only means of preparation, but it was not a good method. Just precisely what would happen was exactly the question for which he could imagine no answer. What *might* happen was as close, he thought, as he could get.

His first thoughts took flight. In her parlor he spilled everything, so that the floor became flooded. The two of them as a result were required to hang upside down by their knees from the ceiling. He hung the lowest, from the end of the chandelier, trying to soak up the mess with a few ineffectual napkins. As they hung, her dress would perhaps begin to fall over her. Lázaro thought to himself, *no.* This was not it.

He took a deep breath, again, and tried to invent something better.

In her parlor she would be invisible. It was her house, after all, and she with her natural grace would fit so well and feel so comfortable. He would be the hippopotamus part of this joke, the hippopotamus with a top hat, the anything-but-invisible.

To Lázaro this awkwardness felt related to the magic act he had seen three years previous on the stage in Nogales. The magician performing had a fool as an assistant. The poor helper, however, was made to be a fool, first by the magician, who kept hitting him over the head with the magic wand. Then the piano player did the work of making things even worse, playing his notes out of tune and louder when the assistant did not see something. The audience had laughed, and then laughed harder.

For all of the making fun, at least the audience allowed the assistant his bow at the end, and his applause. Lázaro thought that no applause would be forthcoming at the end of his own performance. Or else, the clapping would be a sad applause of the circus audience to the old hippopotamus, to the tuskless elephant and the balding tigers. It would be applause, all right, but to cover up the noise of the wish to be elsewhere.

Enough, thought Lázaro. He could not know what would happen when he knocked on her door this next Tuesday. It was enough to know that even one meeting, disastrous or not, would be more than he had earned. That all the parties involved had agreed to a meeting in the first place was still a moment beyond his understanding.

One thanks God at such a moment: this was what Lázaro believed. One lights a candle, or does a good deed—anything to show gratitude, since understanding is not in the cards. Cards served as a good way to think about the whole affair, he decided. He had been dealt the one hand that keeps the men in the Molino Rojo playing cards for life.

LAST TUESDAY AND NEXT Tuesday were one thing. But today was Tuesday Tuesday. Tuesday today. Tuesday now. He had no time left for any of this worrying. He had no time to think about meeting her, yet it was all he could think about. That in itself was something of a marvel, thought Lázaro. What was not possible was all that was possible. He was not sure if he liked this kind of thing.

This thinking was all too much, and he simply stopped himself. His head was all on fire now with this nonsense. His head was filled with too many things to see, filled with invention, with things his eyes had not brought in with them from the outside world. Lázaro hit himself with the flat of his hand on his forehead, like that! A hard one.

He stood dazed. This hit, he thought right away, was the kind that hurts. His head got even hotter, the way a bruise will seem to glow and give off a little of the heat of its color into the surrounding air.

Stupid is another way to think about it, he thought, hitting oneself like that. Even at this Lázaro was ineffectual. There should have been a great deal more pain, the blood of an accident, a limb on the floor at least. Some better proof of good intention. Something worth having done in relation to the torment he was feeling. Something.

He had made The Arrangement last Tuesday, that he would see her Tuesday after next. Today was the Tuesday between, a Tuesday simply named Tuesday, without meaning at all other than being in the middle and having the same name. Still, a rhyme was a rhyme, and should have some meaning. The sounds know something, and say as much to the ears.

Stop. It was time to get on with the business of this day's business. Lázaro told himself this, with force, and took a deep breath. But no more hitting of the head, he decided. Not without something that would show real results. Not without having hit himself with a rolling pin, for example, with which he was familiar, or a cleaver. On thinking this, he decided it was a good thing he was not a butcher.

His was instead the work of a baker. The family bakery, however, had been left to the devices of the Luna women for three generations. So even at this, he felt himself a stranger without map or stars. For as long as anyone could remember, his hands were the first man's to make the morning breads and the Sunday *menudo* in this shop. For that alone he was a curiosity.

The townspeople pretended to look in the bakery window at this sweet bread or that cookie, perhaps an inquiry about when the *pan torcido* would be ready. All the while they were trying to look at him but being polite enough to do nothing that would make him look back.

Their looking was all right most of the time, Lázaro thought. Most of the time he could at least half believe that they might be hungry, and that his were the twisted breads and sweets, the pumpkin *empanadas* of choice.

On this particular Tuesday he was making the *cochitos*. These were the little gingerbread pigs the middle morning rush of *nanas* would buy. They would be shopping for all their stop-crying tricks while the children played in the park. Lázaro was making the *cochitos,* but only more or less today, and some of them did not look like pigs at all. They had begun to look more like watermelons and basketballs, with only halfhearted eyes and incorrectly numbered legs, more like salamanders still forming.

Something in his hands was not working today, something right at that point where one holds the baker's drawing device like a pencil. Today, the forefinger and thumb did not quite have the strength of lines, not of lines that do not wobble as they are drawn. Simply holding those two fingers together hard and with purpose suddenly became on this day the most difficult act in the world.

Doing anything at all of substance at that moment would have been the most difficult of worldly acts. Lázaro wanted only to think of her—but at the same time, he did not. Thinking of her also meant thinking of next Tuesday and what he was going to do, whatever that was. The vague *whatever* made itself alive to Lázaro, and therefore painful.

Seeing her would be pain, he thought, but a good pain, not like hitting oneself on the head. Whatever he was made to go through, he would at least be looking at her. That counted for a great deal, being the careful, one-cup baker's measure against which he could stand a very great amount of pain. A great amount, more or less. He thought again, it was a good thing he was not a butcher.

STARTING FROM THAT MIDDLE Tuesday the *cochitos* began to take on a life of their own, pigs in disguise. It was to the delight of all the children who saw them, who then asked for more, and then more after that. No one pig looked the same as another. The children began to see that they must have the next pig and then the next, the way adults kept going to the movies to see the next chapter and then the next in one of the many long-running Saturday dramas. The pigs in this curious manner began themselves to tell a story in all the ways they kept changing.

The children understood. And they gave over to these pigs all the names they had previously held in trust for various dolls they had hoped to receive—Marvella the queen of all the queens, Dulce who had no mother and did what she wanted, Perfecto who was tall but who came to be always on his stomach, having to give all the others rides, and who finally became a horse but like a weenie dog.

The children began, slowly at first, to get in trouble. They no longer ate these pig cookies straight away, or at all. They first held on to them, and then strapped them to their books and took them to school.

Then the children began to fashion oddities of clothing for the pigs. They made dresses from cupcake papers, tin foil necklaces, a cut-out suit from a large lettuce leaf. The lettuce, however, right away spoiled. Even then, it became a rather handsome brown suit, almost matching the gingerbread color and almost making the doll Perfecto look as if he wore no clothing at all. The children all laughed too hard at the naked Perfecto, and when they were scolded, it gave them time to wonder.

Through all the excitement, through Tuesday and Wednesday and Thursday and the rest, Lázaro took no notice of his newfound fame, though it clearly was a fame. Not until Saturday morning, when the crowd began gathering outside the bakery, did he see that something was the matter. He opened the front door to join the crowd, thinking there might be a fire or some such commotion.

But as he came out, the children in the crowd gathered instead around him. He could make out from all the laughing a single question, though it was being asked in a hundred different ways—what would they do next, Don Lázaro? What will they look like and what will they be saying?

Lázaro looked at the children all around him. He looked at the adults who also gathered but who were pretending to be there almost as if by accident, as if they were simply passing. The baker threw his hands up in the air and made his shoulders say to all of them that he did not understand any of this. He did not know what these little girls were asking, or why these little boys were crying. He did not know why anyone would be holding up, to show him, the hands of one of his little pigs from yesterday—did it in fact have hands?

Lázaro tried to look more closely, but too many children were pressing in too near. What the pig cookie had, did

23

in fact look like hands. He could not imagine from where the hands had come, or why the children would have done such a thing to his pig. The pig he was being shown was not quite right. But here he could see clearly for the first time that the hands did indeed seem to fit.

THEN THE SUNDAY BEFORE The Tuesday, The Tuesday of the Arrangement, an idea came to Lázaro as he was stirring the *cochito* batter. It was now the batter of surprise, as even he had begun to take a good look at what he had been doing. Of course the easiest idea, thought Lázaro, would have been to do something very clever with the pigs. He could have made marvelous, stretched and winged beings inarguably full of love out of the batter and have the children take them over to … he found himself almost saying her name, but caught himself … her house, the children making her look, and upon seeing them she would understand everything so that when he came to her house there would be music and pineapples and laughing and he would find her in his arms, find her eyes in his arms in that way of all dreams. That would be the cleverest idea.

But who knew how to do such tricks? It was the stuff of stories, and Lázaro had no hand in that. His was the lot of cookie maker, among the generations of women, in the shadows of his brothers who took what they wanted.

So his idea of the smart pigs only made Lázaro sadder, knowing that he did not know how to do even an easy thing in this whole affair of the heart. Having thought up the possibility of these ideas made him more afraid as well. Now he would have to face her with even less to his credit than he might have had this coming Tuesday.

Lázaro would have no pigs with hands to explain for him his love of her. He could not, after all, be nearly so blunt himself. He could not do what his cookies could do. They could explain to her. They could tell his desire to see her again, the following Tuesday, and perhaps the Sunday after that, at the concert of clowns in the park, for whom posters were hung already, he himself having put one right on the entryway door to his own shop, a poster of a clown sitting in the mouth of a tiger, the clown with his own mouth open, and in his mouth a small musical note, all on top of an elephant. What music could this be, he had wondered. A song in the mouth of a painted man. His cookies could tell her.

HIS TUESDAY CAME. LÁZARO dressed himself in much the same manner as the making of his pigs, a tie more or less there, a handkerchief around his waist, his trousers more or less raised. His hair had to fend for itself, lucky to have been combed reasonably well the day before. Lázaro knew better than this, but it was all he could manage.

Still, he took with him as well the other things, his shoulders and his stomach and his true eyes. Lázaro wanted for them all to see her, whose name he had no right to say. Lázaro knew her name, but if he were to let his mouth speak it, he knew his mouth would not then let it go.

Lázaro saw himself in the circus poster he had kept in his window.

Today he was coming to ask if she would consent to see him again, only that. The most difficult act in the world, he thought with his stomach, was this first saying of *hello*. This first daring to call, without permission, Desire by its first name.

Waltz of the Fat Man

NOÉ'S HOUSE TRIM WAS painted blue, good blue, deep and neat, with particular attention to the front door, that it should stand against spirits. He kept the house in repair, and each year hired a gardener necessary for the first three seasons—spring and summer, a little while in autumn. In this place it was a gray wind after that, a time for burying things in the ground to save them or to hide them.

His personal appearance suffered nothing from the attentions to his house, as Noé kept on himself a trim moustache and a clean face, neat clothes for which he thanked Mrs. Martínez, patronizing her for a quarter of a century. From ironing his clothing, she knew the shape of his body more than he did, and for her consequent attention to detail in that regard he was appreciative—just the right fold in the collars, a crease moving a little to the left along his right leg, the minor irregularities and embarrassments. And he was doubly thankful as she never said a word to him about it.

His was a body full of slow bones, after all, and he moved as if long fish swam in a small place.

Noé did not think himself fat, but he felt himself heavy, in a manner he could not explain to anyone. His body to be sure was overweight, but he did not feel it to be something of the stomach or thighs; rather, it was a heaviness that came from the inside out, manifesting itself to the world as the body of a fat man.

On his best days, Noé could make that weight look like muscles. On his best days he could make his stomach go into his chest and his shoulders, and people would believe anything he had to say.

Noé had a business as a butcher, but it was too much for him, a sadness cutting the meats. He had become a butcher, after all, purely for social reasons. It was a civic service, and he wanted to do good things. But it was not a good choice, given what he desired, which was simply to be part of the town.

To be sure, people patronized his shop, and took him up on his offer of extra services and niceties, but they did not finally stay very long to talk, not in the way they stayed for coffee and to warm themselves at the baker's. He could see them in there, with their mouths open and their eyes rolling along a line of laughter.

He could not say why the townspeople were like this, exactly. Perhaps it was his full size, or something about his looks, or about being the butcher in a town and being too good at his trade. But the whole of his life was that no one cared much for him, or even spoke to him very much, and when he attended wakes, which he did because he was a courteous man, he left indentations in the kitchen linoleum that would not go away.

Noé knew that, though he tried not to be, in the people's minds he was simply an irritation.

In whatever part of the town he walked, people spoke behind their hands, and pointed when they didn't think Noé could see them. But his eyes were fat as well, and because of that he could see more.

WHEN NOÉ DANCED, HE wore a blue suit, and was always alone, always at the same place outside of town, by the river reeds.

He danced with the wind, which was also cruel like the women of the town, but the wind at least did not have a face. He locked the trunks of his arms with the branch arms of the black walnut trees, which also like the women of the town did not bend around to hold him, did not invite him to another, softer room.

But these arms of a tree could not leave Noé so easily. They could not so quickly give him over cruelly to the half-hot tongues of the weeds so that they might talk about him, and make their disapproving sounds.

When he danced this dance he let out with a small noise his thin girl, which he kept inside himself. This is what had made him look fat, the holding in, the keeping in of the noise inside himself, his desire to freely speak his needs as a human being in the company of other human beings. This was his thin girl.

And Noé would let her out and they would dance the dance of weddings into the night.

NOÉ TOOK TO WEARING his blue suit to the shop, because he thought he looked better. He did this in case someone would look at him, and think the better of him, think him something of a fine man after all.

Then his plan of the blue suit grew into a great deal more, taking as he did the wearing of his suit as some small license. It was the license, he thought, of a regular man. And he tried what he imagined to be the secret work of a regular man in the company of a regular woman.

When he shook the hands of women, he did so vigorously, hoping to see movement on their bodies, some small adventure to take his breath, some nodding yes, some quiet dance of the upper body. This first adventure of a man.

His was a modest plan, and worked a little. The shaking of the hands was, however, the most Noé did. It gave him so much, and he thought the intimate movements of a woman to be so loud, there in front of everybody, that he could go no further.

But that is why Noé attended wakes so faithfully as well, sometimes as if they were the whole of his social life: how in comforting a bereaved wife he could—properly and in front of everyone so that there was no question of propriety— kiss her on the cheek.

Even then, after the hour of praying for the deceased and thinking about what he would do, by the time his moment was at hand, his attempt at kissing was a dizzied missing of the mark, as it had been when he was a boy. His lips to the cheek were so clumsy and so fast that the kiss was more of something else, something not quite anything, something in keeping with his life after all, as it had been and continued to be.

THE BUTCHER SHOP THROUGH the slow years began to change, as did Noé himself. He had taken up in his house the collection and caring of clocks, because, he said to himself, they had hands, and in so many clocks was a kind of heaven, a dream of sounds to make the hours pass in a manner that would allow him to open up shop again the next day.

His nighttime dream became a daytime dream as well. He did not keep them, could not keep the clocks, finally, only at home. Along with Noé in his blue suit, the shop also began to find itself dressed differently, hung with clocks, first one, a plain dark wood, and then two, and then a hundred. Each of them with two hands for him.

There was a blue clock. Cuckoos and 28-day, anniversary clocks to the side of the scale, large-faced numbers where once there had been letters in the sections of an illustrated cow.

What Noé knew and did not say was that in these clocks were the people he knew, that here was the anniversary Mariquita, the schoolhouse Mariette, Marina the singular blue, Caras with her bird tongue. The clock he knew to be Armida had hands that sometimes rose outstretched to the two and ten like the blessing arms of Christ, and sometimes lowered to the five and seven of desire, one hand shorter, in the act of beckoning him, a come here, Noé. A come here, I've got something to tell you, Noé, come on, don't be afraid.

This was no butcher shop, the townspeople would say to themselves, not with clocks. One or two clocks maybe, but not so many as this. It would not have been so bad, except that he was the only butcher in town, and people had to make use of his services. An unofficial inquiry was opened as to whether or not there was perhaps a law, some ordinance, prohibiting such abuses of the known world, but no one could find any reference that applied to the walls of a butcher shop, other than cleanliness. And of that, there could be no discussion. Noé did not neglect the clocks, and therefore did not neglect the white-sheeted bed of his walls.

ONE EVENING IN WINTER as Noé was closing up his shop, having wound the clocks for the night and having left just enough heat in the stove that they would not suffer, he heard the blue clock falter. So much like a heartbeat had the sounds of the clocks come to be for him, that he was alarmed and stumbled in his quickness to reach the clock, though it could not move and was not falling. It called to him none-theless as a wife in pain might call to her husband: *honey,* it said, *please.*

He reached it too late, he thought, though it was simply a clock, and he laughed at himself.

He tried winding the clock again, thinking the unthinkable, that perhaps he had missed its turn in his haste to leave. But that was not it: the spring was taut, and there was no play.

He took it down from its nail, and looked at it from different angles in his hands, but he could see nothing extra-ordinary. There was no obvious damage, no one had dropped it without telling him and rehung it, no insect had been bor-ing into its side. Its blue was still blue, without blemish.

He took it to the counter and measured out some butcher's paper in which to wrap it, deciding that he would take it home to see to its difficulty. He put string around it and made a good blanket of the paper, which should comfort, he always said, what was inside. As he picked it up he could hear the workings move, and he resolved to be wary of its delicacy. He need not have done it, yet he warned himself anyway, as if he were his own mother.

He put the clock in the crook of his arm, closed and locked his door, took a deep breath in the cold air, hunched his shoulders and began his walk toward home.

He had errands, but they could wait. And he was, in any event, the last of the merchants to close for the evening, so he would have been out of luck anyway. Save for the clock, this was how his evenings most often came to an end, the closing of the door and the walk toward home.

An occasional voice greeted him, and he returned the hello, but it was the conversation of single words, friendly enough, and that was all.

SOME THEORIZED LATER IT was the soldiers who were common in those days and who hung around with nothing better to do, that it was they who had been paid, because they never did anything for nothing, but would do anything for something, those soldiers from that kind of army.

There was nothing tragic, of course, nothing for which any charges could be drawn, in much the same manner that nothing could be legally said about what Noé had done to his butcher's shop. You get back what you give, someone was later reported as having said, someone but not anyone in particular. That's how it was told to the captain of the police.

Noé was walking home with his package, which no one could have known was the blue clock. No one but perhaps the soldiers, and only then if they had been nosy enough to have been watching through his window, which had been recently broken and was full of cardboard patches, easy enough to hide behind.

The package's aspect was of a ham or a roast of some sort, a good rabbit, something simple and natural in the arm of a big man walking home to dinner.

Darkness had set and the moon was new. He cast no shadow and made his way quickly as he left the last of the downtown buildings. The ground was neither muddy nor dry, resembling something closer to a woody mulch, and through him passed a moment of gardens from sometime in his life, gardens he had passed through, or that his mother had kept. It was a simple feeling, and brought a prickling to his skin.

He next passed by the stand of walnut trees and wild oleander which was white-flowered in the summer.

The oleander called to him, *Noé*.

At first it was so quiet he said to himself he did not hear it, *Noé*.

Noé, the oleanders said, louder this time, and he stopped to look. Though it was dark and the moon was hidden, he was not afraid.

His size was such that he had never been made to be afraid, not at a moment like this. It was, if one could read his face, a curiosity, this sound which was reminiscent of his name. It was like the mulch and his mother's garden, and it gave him a prickling of the skin once more.

Noé. He heard it again, and stopped, and turned to it, asking who was there, what did they want, that perhaps he could be of some service.

No one answered, so he reached his free hand into the leaves and moved them around. He heard the sound and then saw what seemed like, in the dimness, a rabbit, running into the underbrush.

Ha, he said, and let it go. He turned again to walk, pulling his coat back up onto his neck.

Noé. It was a whisper, this time he was sure. Not a voice, but more of a breath. A half-breath, but unmistakable in its enunciation.

As a child, Noé might have crossed himself, and as he was sometimes his own mother, he had the impulse, but he just stood there, once more.

He put down the clock in order to enter the oleander more fully, and see what was what, but he found nothing, only branches and the small noises of startled birds and lizards.

When he came out he could not find his package, though he concentrated with his eyes and with his hands. It was not there.

A voice whispered once more, *Noé. You know me,* it said, *you know who I am.*

Noé no longer moved around. He listened, and he waited.

Noé. He did know the whisper. He had in fact heard it many times. He knew the whisper more than the voice of his neighbor, whom he had seen a thousand times.

He would not have believed any of it had this not been the blue clock. Marina his blue, who had made so many places for herself in his life. Not big places, but so many, her hair color on the trim of his house, the color of her eyes in his suit. She was the blueness inside him, the color of his appetite, the color both of what filled him and what he needed more of.

Marina, he said.

Noé.

He stood there and waited.

Do you love me?

Noé did not answer.

You can love me if you love me like a horse, said the whisper. *Can you be a horse, Noé? Can you show me how you are a horse?*

Noé stood there, quietly.

He stamped his foot, gingerly at first, unsure and sure at the same time.

Is that it, Noé, is that all the horse you are?

Noé stamped his foot harder, and made a noise with his nose, and partway through his mouth.

Yes, Noé. And are you more of a horse still?

If this were anything but his blue clock, Marina, he would have gone, and given the moment up as the ghosts of this place. Or children, or who knew what. But he could not.

And then he heard the laughter of the soldiers as they could no longer contain themselves, camouflaged so well otherwise in the oleanders. He heard the laughter, but did not bother with it. He turned and went home, without the clock.

HE HAD GONE AWAY from home once before, from his family. He had to. One thing and another, right or wrong, these things didn't matter. It was simply too much to stay.

He had in some manner become an exponent to a regular number. He was ordinary times ten or times twenty, always too much. And his desire carried an exponent as well. He wanted everything to be nice, to be only the Golden Rule, but times ten, and that is too much. He had no sense of himself, and yet he was everything. In that sea of mathematics he had drowned a sailor's death.

And now he had to go away again. The tide had come up, and caught him once more. He sold what was left of his business at a loss to Mr. Molina, who had a scarred face and who wanted to do the work. There was an art in the cutting, and it took Noé, because he was a courteous man, the afternoon to teach the profession's immediate intricacies to Mr. Molina, who had had no idea there was so much to know.

And that same night Noé bought a brown horse and rode it as far into the following days and weeks, as far into the future as he could because he could not wait to see what was there. He arrived at the circus, and in it he made his life again.

But he almost did not make it. A man and a sparrow—each puts a shoulder to the wind, each to his own intention: a sparrow to fly, a man to run. Noé on this night was in between, and even with his weight he felt himself lifted, as if he were in league with angels at the edge of heaven, not quite deserving, but sneaking in with some help through a back door, hoping to go unnoticed again, as he had felt when he had come to this town. But it was not heaven, this place.

He stopped because the circus people were the first to wave him down, all of them standing near the road, as if this were the place, and they knew him, and they had been waiting, and what took him so long, had he not heard them calling into the night for him?

But they had called him without telegraph or telephone. Something stronger.

His moustache curled up from the wind and his body, which had sometimes seemed fat, was hardened, tense in that moment from the cold which had made him hold his breath and flex his muscles for the whole distance of the ride.

He arrived as a beast, almost, something crazed and unshaven, out of breath.

Or as a beast on top of a man, as if the horse itself were more human, and asking for help.

His was a body full of slow bones still, but if it had taken his lifetime up to now to be slow, now the other foot was coming down, and it was fast.

It was the other half of himself now, for the rest of

his years.

This was, after all, the place. And in that moment of dust kicked up and of noise, he began his real career, this life with a whole company of half-size men, two-bodied women, and all the rest of the animals who danced.

The Great Gardens of Lamberto Diaz

A person did not come to these gardens of Lamberto Diaz to admire them or simply to breathe them in. No. One was breathed in by them, and something more. In this place a person was drawn up as if to the breast of the gardens, as if one were a child again, and being drawn up was all that mattered and meant everything.

That's the kind of thing Lázaro Luna always said. It sounds like him all right, the townspeople nodded. And though nobody here ever understood Lázaro Luna one way or the other, that never stopped him from going right ahead and talking some more like this anyway.

People laughed at Lázaro Luna, but they didn't laugh too much. After a while, they would all nod their heads in a kind of understanding, a something more or less, as they would leave a conversation with him and go out the door.

Well, they nodded amongst themselves, what he said about the gardens was true, at least. There was something about the gardens. That much was true. They didn't laugh at Lázaro so much about this.

There was something.

Everyone could see in the gardens how everything there was in motion, reaching into and through the night, everything to its purpose. All the more arresting, these gardens were such an overpowering assemblage of Nature's industry that there was a *hum,* a humming, something born of the vegetable electric.

Stepping inside the gardens, one could feel immediately a great working chicago of purposeful tangle, a choreography, of a thousand paws and pathways of smooth work, of chlorophyll and water and small egg deliveries, of pollen in all manner of transportation. Even the rotting fit in, its color not out of place. Here, every part of the painter's palette found employment, and had meaning.

THE GARDENS HAD STARTED as something quite modest, but then they got away. Lamberto Diaz, the owner of this land, had planned a simple sight, something frivolous to see through the panes of the front kitchen window. Bright colors come as something from the good side of life, Lamberto would say. This was something he had heard Lázaro Luna say, and—because he could not forget it—Lamberto Diaz took the phrase for his own.

A few zinnias, some snapdragons. Things that could manage more or less by themselves. And a little rosemary, because Lamberto Diaz was, in spite of his caprice, a practical man at heart, and could not venture too far without purpose. An herb here or there, he thought, what could it hurt. Something practical, though it was small, helped his whole endeavor make more sense to the town as well, which wondered about such things.

However, by some combination of circumstance, some X-marks-the-spot of fate, in tandem with a previously undiscovered natural spring and a protective roughness of landscape, odd escarpments from the centuries of slowly running water in this place forming cover from the otherwise

harsh winds, and perhaps formed by the winds themselves—
in all of this a garden will grow.

The few zinnias became quickly enough a few thousand, and grew in their happiness to the size of sunflowers.
The sunflowers themselves grew to the size of pumpkins, with
stalks equal to the task. The snapdragons grew ominous, and
the rosemary formed a fragrant carpet more than a mile
square, and strong.

Lamberto Diaz did not know what to do about this
reckless land, and tried not to think about the garden-now-
gardens. They were there, and that was all. He paid no attention, turning himself to the real work that kept his
household, his work in leather, for shoes, and boots, for
purses. Real work in the real world. He paid no attention—
or tried to pay no attention—to the gardens. Ignoring them
was all he could do. That, and wonder why he had ever paid
any attention at all to Lázaro Luna in the first place.

Yet every now and then, though he tried not to,
Lamberto Diaz caught the strains of some kind of music,
sometimes harmonies, or half-strains he thought he could recognize. The sounds scared him, and he always put a pillow to
his head at night. Still, he could not stop himself from following along what the gardens had begun. The songs invariably took him to childhood, or to love. And from there, he
knew, came the inside push toward dance.

Lamberto Diaz was not the only one. These songs
also drew other people to the edge of the gardens, and sometimes into them. They also heard the songs. Not the same
songs, but something. A humming. A humming they had
heard before.

So many bees, they would say to keep themselves out of the gardens, bees and wasps, the sounds of moths, the general sway of the leaves. That is a music after all, they said. That is what they were hearing. And everyone would have to agree. Who, after all, was not that romantic? Who could not agree that the air made its own song?

But what came from the gardens was not finally that earthly music of bees and of leaves. Not after all. It was just what people said to explain themselves, in order not to say that they recognized everything the garden said.

These gardens were not a place to be happy, but one could not be unhappy here. These gardens were simply these gardens, people said. Life is sometimes like that. It doesn't explain.

LAMBERTO DIAZ HAD BOUGHT the land on the advice of young Mr. Lázaro Luna, who had in those early years been a wild young man, but not crazy. Maybe even smart, people said, but not to his face, as he would never let them forget it.

Lázaro had spent a good deal of time walking about on the original scrub land, which then had been useless and altogether ugly. That it was disagreeable explained Lázaro's attraction to this area, at least inasmuch as the town was concerned.

He's that way, they said. *If it adds up to nothing, he's the first one in line with a cup to borrow some.* And it was true that he was the only one to walk in that direction, nobody else seeing any point.

The land cost Lamberto Diaz very little because of the way that it looked: it was untillable and ungrazeable, with too many ragged edges and pitfalls. It was not predictable land, nor measurable, so that the town surveyor had paid it slight attention. On the first several maps of the town, before the gardens, and even long afterward, this area did not exist. The town's surveyor more or less stretched the edges of the surrounding flat land that he had in fact been able to measure, so that these edges joined, leaving this area invisible and unaccounted for.

Lamberto Diaz did not complain, as it saved him money in taxes, and still he was able to walk there. This land was like something in a person's pocket: there and not there, especially if one used only eyes to see.

The escarpments looked like great scars in the body of the ground, and there were probably many acres of land here, but it all went up and down, or around and into a twist, completing some parabolic dimension then without description in science.

It was what it was, and that was the thing, Lázaro said. In extremity there is something, in wildness. He couldn't say what, exactly, just that it was his general feeling about things. Something this ugly, he said, surely there is a use for it equal to the force of its face.

But no one had thought of one. Though in fact, this enigmatic sector of land had become the center of a popular pastime: the more that people tried to describe the land, the more they failed, so then the harder they tried, and failed again. They continued until no more beer was left to be drunk, or lemonade, if it were a birthday party and the people were children.

Even the surveyor's adopted little boy, Tavo, tried to explain it, though his father would not. It was as if, said

Tavo—who was confused in other things, but not in this—it was as if all the edges of the otherwise flat land had their corners here. It all looked like the inside of a pair of pants, full of loose threads and mismatched ends, the parts one was not supposed to look at.

His father was the surveyor, it was true, but his mother was a seamstress, and this sometimes helped him understand the world more, the world and himself, and his confusions with it. These gardens were a place that made sense.

In fact, by so much rolling and sudden movement, so much ground waving and rocking of landscape, it was as if this little valley had a magic wand from the circus waved over it, at what would otherwise have looked like an extensive and bearsome flatness of surrounding land. It was as if the magic wand woke up the land, making it stand and sit and lie, making it do tricks instead of letting it sleep.

The land was made to use the *energy* of its former flatness, and not the weight of the flatness itself, a great energy in service to its own needs. This floridness, this moving land, itself wand-like and whip-like, this edenic corner that did not exist, this venial lie of the maps, this invisible half mile might, like the ringmaster's flat top hat, in truth be many miles long, were it to be popped out on a thigh.

In truth, a simple memory of a grandmother's backyard garden, the old kind, might have been equal to everything people described this place to be, all tinged with a quality of sweetness and reverie. On the other hand, a person did not wake up from this place: it was there. And sweetness and reverie was something people ascribed to memory, not the present. So these gardens made them nervous.

THE GARDEN GREW OUT of the bare land not without help. People took things there.

A few nameless exotic and random seedlings, items garnered from the passing trains, which carried forward only those parts of their cargo that were perfect. Anything otherwise—a sprouted seed where all others were dormant—got left along the way. Sometimes these imperfect or impatient plants constituted a gift, or *mordida,* to the railway inspector, who would be cheerful at the inducement to let slip a minor regulation or two. He would be pleased, if surprised, by the gift of seeds clandestinely put in his hand. But he didn't know what to do with them after a while.

Others in town had their own versions of why they brought offerings to the edge of the gardens and threw them in as well. Old pots and dried petals began to give a curious aspect to the gardens. People saw different features in the affluent tangle. Because each had contributed something, even a great deal, to the growing of the gardens, each saw what was there in terms of his own life.

Each of the townspeople who came out to the gardens remembered what each had put in. Over time, they all began to think of themselves as the secret author of the gardens, appropriating unto themselves all the rest of the flora as the natural outgrowth of their original contribution.

Each time the old baker came out here, she would find herself in front of what she thought to be a tremendous field of bread, with cakes and biscuits, *cochitos* and twisted French breads, everything from her shop suddenly wild in nature, wild and big, so that she could see into them, see the ingredients themselves, marjoram and yeast gone wild, a great ton of gathered yeasts, moving, with singular faces half happy and half drowning in the goat milk and sweet waters. So much cinnamon and ginger, the slow cardamom and the whistling chile seasonings, the white sorcerer powders traditional of cooks, the seeds and the sprinkles. All of it gathered, as if for some tremendous wedding, some coronation. The gardens in this way made the baker happy, something so big, and all hers.

Sometimes, the gardens were a convenient place to discard even those things that were not flora. But it didn't stop the contributor from feeling any less the covert landlord of this place.

The butcher when he came to stand here saw all the parts of his trade that he had tossed in over the years gathered again, reassembled into what he suspected in his nightmares: some monstrous cow with the hooves of a goat, all the parts of all the animals he had touched with his hands and with his steel, all of it bleeding, all of it lowing and shivering, all of it beautiful in its drum-and-bugle, band-like quality of color and clean slices, all of it damnation, but all of it in the necessary and honorable service to a small town, and in that way something of joy.

These were flowers and plants, trees and vines. But everyone in town saw them as something like buttons or teeth, as carded wool and apple hearts.

Except Lázaro Luna, who held none of these jobs. Or rather, he had held them all, but only for a little while. In this way, the garden for him was doubly a garden, and triply, for there was no end to how he saw this place.

WHILE WATCHING THE GARDEN get bigger and then wider, it was Lázaro Luna's habit to stand himself on the edge of any of the many precipices and to urinate himself out, extending some inside part of himself in that stream, extending it out, over, and down into the vastness. Lázaro came to think of the many thousand foot fall of his urine as flight, as himself flying, as if either this stream of himself were going very far down and he were at a great height, or else he himself was in the very act of rising. The feeling made him stretch his arms sometimes. Sometimes he would wave, one arm going up wildly, as if he were a rodeo rider there on the edge of the world.

This drama of standing on the ledges of the garden became his habit, and he sometimes contributed more or less of himself to the vastness. In this way Lázaro believed himself to be the keeper of the garden, the true gardener—more or less, depending on his day and his mood, and the extent of his contribution.

What occurred to him regularly was that his addition to the gardens was an imperfection. But urine was a perfect carrier of imperfection, a good trick of the body. In the same manner, according to the prevailing notion of proper uses for land, so was a garden an imperfection, useless for cattle or for crops, but perfect in its imperfection, with bright color and bright smell. It was a good trick, a good trick on the land, or of the land. Sometimes, he thought, a stretch of land must simply have to flower or die. It was something he could understand.

That urinating simply and with shuddering felt good, Lázaro could not begin to address. Except in that it all described his life, he thought. His was a life of small adventures. Lázaro was never, and never would be, anything—not with regard to any job description this town would recognize.

He was not a lawyer or a farmer.

He was a baker now, to be sure, no longer an apprentice, but he knew he would find something else. Lázaro had been everything in this town, for a little while. He even felt himself becoming something else just by watching, and had in that way thought himself to be the town butcher for a few weeks, such a study had he made at the window of the butcher's shop. Not that he practiced what he saw—just that he could do anything was something he believed.

BUT FOR ALL LÁZARO'S watching of the doings of the world, one day someone instead saw him. Saw him as he stood on the edge of the particular day's precipice and let himself fly over it in his small way. Saw Lázaro because there he was, for all the world to see, with his pants in disarray, and who knew what else, as was later said.

Not that anyone cared too much. Peeing into a big hole in the ground. Who wouldn't, after all, given half a chance. Or rather, who had not, after all. So that was not the news, not the news exactly.

The real news was the stream of liquid itself, or what it looked like, half in the sun and half in the thousand three-quarter shadows of where it was going.

On this day and at the angle of sight crucial to the moment, his stream of liquid reflected light and deflected light, it broke light and scattered light, it bent light and pulled it—so much inside himself had Lázaro stored up for this moment on this Saturday.

So much had he accumulated that, as he let go, it was a thicker and richer stream than normal. It was for the garden, and like the garden.

Not at all something from the common. This outpouring was from the moment when one has waited and waited and now can wait no longer and just in time has come to the moment of relief so that there occurs a small explosion and a small outrage and a small joy of urine as if one had let a thousand schoolchildren out of a classroom at once.

This kind of relieving of oneself after so long was from that moment when a man is still like a horse.

Because of this, because of the thickness and the fullness of this rope of water, Mrs. Calderón, who was at some distance, could not in fact tell where Mr. Lázaro Luna's actual body part ended, and where the liquid began.

In fact, it seemed to her at that moment that Mr. Lázaro Luna's particular body part did not end; that in his hand he held something that did not stop; that out of his pants he had unrolled a mighty who-knew-what, an elephant's trunk, five, and then ten elephant's trunks, so that she turned her eyes away, and she ran back to town. She had an education, after all, and knew better than to stare for too long.

But this was indeed a man who was a horse. She knew animals, and had seen a horse come out of himself down there between the legs, looking long enough to be impossible, capable almost of reaching across the entire corral. Lázaro Luna standing there and holding himself in his hand looked just like this, like a horse. What she saw at that moment was perhaps a trick of light and of angle, but she did not think so: with her own eyes it looked like Lázaro Luna's most private part was half a mile long.

BUT HOW TO DELIVER such news is difficult to figure, and Mrs. Calderón didn't know what to do.

She arrived at the first of the shops ready to shout, but could not find an appropriate word equal in evocation to *fire!* or *circus!*

Even as she caught her breath and bent herself down with her hands on her thighs tired from running, neither could she think of a string of words, a phrase, something for those things that take longer to describe—*the wind! it's the wind! and it's lifted sheep into the air! run!* Nothing like that.

All she could say at the first shop, a shop for sewing and material, but not large like the mercantile, was *Lázaro Luna!*

The two young women inside, after listening, rolled their eyes. Yes, they both said, first with their eyes and then with their mouths, almost in unison, *Lázaro Luna.*

You should have known, the two women said. *Hasn't Lázaro Luna been in too many conversations already, enough so that anyone should know?*

They both nodded their heads, as if putting up their hands and saying what was one to do. But even with their declarative nodding they knew full well that, since Mr. Luna was neither married nor ugly—just what he was each young woman kept to herself—he would not be leaving the corral of their conversations any time soon.

So, they found no surprise at this breathless Mrs. Calderón, whose first words were Lázaro Luna's name. They had felt much the same way themselves, and more than once. That Mrs. Calderón was *Mrs.* Calderón, well. They understood—it was unfair, but they understood. Lázaro, after all, knew things. Nobody could argue that.

Nothing bad. Quite the contrary. Everything he knew was good. Good for everyone. That was the problem.

He was at the gardens, said Mrs. Calderón, in her next breath. The two young women looked at each other. When was he not at the gardens?

He was at the great gardens, and with his pants down. Well, they nodded. That was Lázaro Luna all right. They said it more as a sigh. In that sigh as well was the small question of who it was this time that was there with him.

But in his hand, she said, still out of breath. Her listeners were eager now.

Yes? they both said. *In his hand?*

Yes, said Mrs. Calderón. *Exactly. In his hand.*

So the afternoon began, and the next installment on a Lázaro Luna story. He was more entertainment than anything else in town, all by himself. Everyone was in agreement on that.

And in such a context, finding out that popular and daring Mr. Luna was, perhaps, a horse—well, that would explain a great deal.

LÁZARO LUNA HAD NOT seen Mrs. Calderón. He simply finished his chore, pulled up his pants, and continued his walk.

He felt good being so filled in his body and alive that he had needed to relieve himself with such urgency.

He felt good as he relieved himself, as if the process itself were some kind of matchless gift.

And he felt good that he had relieved himself, as who would not. There was nothing left to do but whistle, to pick up the small melody of the green, to try and carry its song for a while into the morning.

It was joy that he felt. And joy was what he wanted from the gardens, something of them to transfer into him. For them to become him in some way. If it had worked with his father and with sadness in some of his later days, could the idea of contagion not also work with these gardens and with that which was not sadness? He set about probing his theory as if he were a scientist, which he was on some days.

AND ON SOME DAYS he was not a scientist. Some days he was simply Lázaro Luna, and nothing more. He did not have theories then, only desires.

That a garden should grow here had not been his original intent in getting Lamberto Diaz to buy this land. He had simply hoped for a private place to walk, or to walk with someone.

Lamberto Diaz listened to him and his advice to buy the land. Lázaro felt certain he would get a general permission to be on the premises any time he wanted if Lamberto Diaz bought it, and such was the case. Lamberto Diaz, as did the rest of the town, liked as an entertainment to imagine something of the life of Lázaro Luna, so he was happy to give permission, hoping to help in any way he could.

Whether Lázaro actually lived the life everyone imagined for him was certainly not something Lázaro would talk about himself. But he did not mind that everyone else had so much to say about it.

That a garden flourished, and that the single garden became many gardens—well, that also became part of the story of Lázaro Luna. *Whatever he touched,* they would say. *There he would find a garden.*

No one was quite sure just what that meant, but they said it anyway, and with pleasure.

IT MIGHT HAVE BEEN joy that Mrs. Calderón carried away from her encounter with Lázaro Luna at the precipice of the gardens, though she could not recognize it at first. But after a while, she saw how the talk about what she had beheld made everyone happier, because they laughed.

Who could talk about this, after all? On the other hand, who could not talk about this? So she did. She, Mrs. Calderón, with her own eyes had seen everything, she said to those who had begun to gather.

But wasn't there the bonus of wondering what Mrs. Calderón was doing looking at Lázaro Luna to begin with, they said to her, and laughed even harder.

Just walking, she had said. *I was just walking.* But who could get away with an answer like that except Lázaro Luna, even if it were true?

It's just that I heard a kind of music, she insisted. And in that, everyone knew, there was some truth. They all knew the gardens. So the matter of her part in all of this was dropped. More or less. There was not much to explain. Sometimes the gardens simply called a person, and that was that.

Anyway, as long as she kept talking about Lázaro Luna, people questioned her own part in this less and less. As long as she had a little more to say each time. And she did.

The story got so big finally, over a period of several days, that it reached Lázaro Luna himself. Someone had left a little of the story on a plaza bench, another had laughed a little too hard at something Lázaro had said, and another had shaken his hand, forcefully, but for no reason, there on the sidewalk in front of the shops.

In the way that Lázaro did not simply use his eyes to see things, neither did he simply use his ears for listening.

In the next few days, as he walked himself toward the gardens, he noticed on his way out of town just how many people were noticing him, taking some extra time to wave or to smile. More noticeably, he began to see how many of them were gathering at the sewing shop, last along the row of stores at the end of town. One might think this sewing shop had become a café, something French, something from another place, thought Lázaro.

So of course he went in.

Well, it's not true, certainly not, he said, as he readied himself to leave, and pretended to adjust his pants. He said it without a hint of a laugh. So everyone else laughed.

A horse, how could it be? What a shame Mrs. Calderón is not here. Of course I would have to find some way to convince her. He put his hand to his chin as if to consider the point.

Lamberto Diaz, who happened to be there, offered to make Lázaro a saddle for his back. There was more laughter, and Lázaro suggested that perhaps they would all like to accompany him on his morning walk and see for themselves. Then they could report back to Mrs. Calderón and make things right in the world.

Lázaro winked at Lamberto. It meant something strong between them, but the wink also meant something to everyone else as well. Seeing a wink is as strong as getting one. The obvious thing was that of course Lamberto Diaz himself had already seen Lázaro Luna, maybe swimming, or bathing, and that now the truth was out.

There was more laughter, and they all shook their heads *no, thank you.*

Of course, the gardens make you see things, said Lázaro. *If that is true, perhaps what I've been looking at all this time is untrue. Perhaps Mrs. Calderón is correct. Do you think it's possible?*

The two young women who worked in the shop shook their heads *no,* but not without looking at each other and smiling.

They shook their heads not because they did not believe Lázaro. It was just that everyone knew he could not be trusted, that one should never take him at his word quite, and that the opposite of what he said was, on the average, more true. Lázaro never told the truth, not exactly. The truth of it was, Lázaro simply never told anyone much about anything he did. He kept in himself a room, and in there things happened. But nobody could see.

That was the thing.

The two young women looked at each other. Looking straight at each other was all they could do with their eyes, because their eyes would not otherwise behave themselves.

Everyone in the store got up and went about the business of the day, and Lázaro went on his walk, and the day went forward.

Forward, more or less. In an effort to seem calm and assuaged, they all had run out so quickly on the pretense of regular business that, filled with so many earnest people moving so quickly, the day more or less tilted over, tripped, and fell onto itself, getting up as the next morning, when everyone gathered again in the sewing shop, because how could they not?

They gathered as quickly as possible, but all without Lázaro Luna this time, because how could they talk about him if he kept interrupting the conversation, which is what they knew he would do. Lázaro had that habit. Just to be sure, they all sat at the window in the event that he might come by.

So, they all agreed, because how could one afford not to believe something as startling as this? Theirs was a progressive town, after all, and they all had open minds which, they agreed, should be open to new ideas. It's what all the best towns were doing.

So, they all agreed, noting that Lázaro had denied everything, and made them laugh in the way that he always did. *So,* they said, and nodded their heads because they knew all along, and because they knew how life worked around here, *so it's true what they say about Lázaro Luna.*

So, they said, and then after a while became quiet. In that quiet inside each of them Lázaro Luna walked, again. And in that quiet, which grew larger like the gardens, Lázaro needed more room than before. With his elbows and his feet, Lázaro pushed the sides of this quiet until it fit him, big, and according to his needs.

And in the quiet, which was bigger than the room now, there was a *hum.*

So, they said, or rather would have said, had the quiet not entirely taken them over.

Exhausted from this talk and from so much laughter, Lamberto Diaz finally slapped his hand on a table, and said good-bye to them all. *And get out of here, all of you hangers-on. Look at us all, riders of Mr. Horse-in-his-Pants. Of course he's a horse. He's a very good horse. And I am going to let him ride me home.*

That's how Lamberto Diaz left, and why he walked down the street in that funny way he did. He stirred up the air from one end of town to the other, using Lázaro Luna's name as a stick.

It worked, because everyone turned to look at him. Or if Lázaro Luna's name was not a stick, as it did not hit anyone directly on the head, then it was a single but strong good oak oar, so that it could not help but make the boat of this world turn around.

Lamberto Diaz spun himself dizzy, and fell in a heap to the ground, until Lázaro himself came to him, and helped him up, and took him to the far side of town where the two of them drank the hundred beers a story like this, a story with arms and with legs and with horses, makes easy, makes swim into the water of the night.

THOUGH HE INVARIABLY FOUND the garden and the music and the greenness, Lázaro Luna did not always find them in the manner they imagined. A garden after all is many things.

Lázaro many years later waited with Lamberto Diaz in the government clinic. Lamberto Diaz had a long series of sporadic heart attacks, between which he sometimes gained an active consciousness.

During one such juncture, he looked up at Lázaro, and with a showman's gesture of the two hands—both thrown into position as if to say *ta da* —he did in fact say to Lázaro, *ta da, I'm having a heart attack.*

Lázaro would remember how Lamberto Diaz said it, not to call Lázaro to his side, as one would call a doctor, with an exclamation point. Rather, he said it in the way that during a parade a father might point out something of particular interest to his son.

I'm having a heart attack, Lamberto Diaz said again, smiled, and lost his eyes to some other consciousness.

What he had wanted to say is what Lázaro heard: this is a heart attack, my friend. Don't be afraid.

Lázaro would remember how he and Lamberto Diaz sat there together the two of them until Lamberto died, an hour later. There were people around, a doctor, whose name Lázaro would not recall, a nurse, and so on. But it was just the two of them, for an hour. The two of them and everything.

All Lázaro could do was to tell Lamberto Diaz about the gardens, and to hum a little of what he had heard there. And all Lamberto Diaz could do was listen.

LÁZARO IN LAMBERTO DIAZ'S last minutes began to feel as if his own mouth were Lamberto Diaz's mouth, and the words it made were Lamberto Diaz's words, so close were the two of them at that moment and in that place. In the same way that Lázaro thought himself a part of the gardens, so did Lázaro Luna find himself to be a part of this man, this friend from a long time.

They simply fit together now, one necessary to the other. In this there was a kind of love. For this reason, Lázaro Luna had to talk, so that Lamberto Diaz would keep talking. The more Lázaro talked, the more right and normal the moment would be, in the midst of a world where nothing else was right.

Everything else was in fact altogether wrong, the world at that moment and in that place, wrong to the point of scandal. Lázaro Luna knew for a fact that Lamberto Diaz weighed more than this. The hand that Lázaro held at that moment in his own weighed nothing, and did not even move the way a hand moves, nor did it look the way a hand should look.

It was a substitution, low quality, and should have been obvious to any of the staff had they bothered to look. Someone as well had stolen part of Lamberto's face in this clinic. There should be laws, thought Lázaro. Laws against this kind of thing, not just for the taking of wallets.

Lázaro saw Lamberto's tongue, or what should have been his tongue, but in its place was some kind of eel from the marketplace, something just lurking there in the quiet, hoping not to be seen. And Lamberto's fingers, thought Lázaro, they should not be able to twist all the way around.

Lázaro tried to say something about this to Lamberto, but Lamberto shushed him. *You don't look so well yourself,* Lamberto managed, *so don't talk about me.*

And Mother of God don't talk to me about body parts, Mr. Horse-in-his-Pants. Don't think anybody will forget something like that.

They laughed together, but in that laugh Lamberto Diaz gave everything left of himself to Lázaro.

That moment of everything transferred from the fullness of Lamberto Diaz's body something to Lázaro Luna's face, the moment finding itself embodied in the full, quiet sounds of Lázaro's suddenly hard mouth and large eyes.

As he hummed to Lamberto, Lázaro thought there is a music in a government clinic too, but it tries to enter one through the wrong places, through the closed line of the mouth and the corners of the eyes. Never the ears, and never straight in front. That's why one must pay attention.

The music here was the movement in a symphony orchestra from strings to woodwind, until all of the sounds were wood. But here the crowd gave no *aplauso* for the performers. This thing of sadness and crowds did not say everything about the wandering presence and grand performance of sorrow.

Thinking this made Lázaro remember how, several times at night in play and without clothes next to a woman and without thinking, Lázaro had for a time begun to say something like, *ha, ahá, there Saturnino, there magnífico, there,* to make the woman laugh. *Not exactly a horse,* he would say, *like I know you've heard. An elephant maybe.* The woman would laugh harder.

Perhaps this is why I never married, thought Lázaro. A sadness would sometimes come over him in that moment with a woman, and he had to say something else. Sometimes he did not feel like Lázaro the horse or Lázaro the elephant, and he would become quiet. Even then, he could not escape from himself or the laughter. There is something loud inside quietness, he would think.

It was like the gardens this way, in that the gardens took from the flatness of the surrounding land the very energy of flatness, and turned it around into something else. In this way, Lázaro Luna never quite knew where he belonged, or which he loved better, the flat or the green, the laughter or the quiet.

And the woman would laugh anyway.

But then so would he, and that was the thing.

With a sparkle of his eye, which in this government clinic was the same as laughter, as good as laughter, he said good-bye to his friend Lamberto Diaz.

Trains at Night

MR. LEE, AS HE transferred chicken feed from the large bin to his everyday pitcher, noticed how the dust rose from the seeds, how steam rises from a landscape, cold, or hot from a white cup of *café con leche,* how smoke rises from a casual back-yard fire, how a soul is given up from a sick man. He did not take meaning from this, it was not instruction to him. He simply saw it.

However, when the soldiers came, he had wished possession of that capability, of effecting a rising beyond his own body, of leaving it for them to take, and thereby not feeling what they would do to him, which was unimaginable.

He saw the moment of his imagined escape everywhere, in everything, in the rising of smoke from a cigarette, in a flock of sparrows taking flight. Even, he thought, in the sound of a song let go from the mouth, a whistled aria. That a note of music should take its rightful place with the birds.

He wished it equally for all of them, but his wish did not work very well. The soldiers rounded up all the Chinese they could find, in a day and a night, without warning or manners, without explanation, by neighbor's direction and by rumor and by store sign. Who could have thought this is what would happen, said the townspeople afterward.

But a soldier is a soldier, and who could say no to a soldier's voice? A brown suit like that takes a man, and turns him into his parts. He is nobody's son anymore.

They are always there, without birth and without death, these soldiers. Nobody could say where a soldier comes from. Or who his teachers are, or what they must look like. Where are manners such that a loud step, a stiff neck, a salute in place of the rightful shaking of a hand are marks of grace? Without the hand offered, where is the chance of agreement? Where is the chance of understanding what another has been through by the feeling of roughness in his palm?

MR. LEE WAS MARRIED with his body and in his heart for a thousand years to Jesusita, married because of, he would shrug his shoulders, who can say? It was like the workings, the intestines, of an opera, he would suggest, and were they not, the two of them, worthy singers in the plot? She would shake her head at him and say she did not understand.

But she did. Not in the way he said it, but she understood in some other way, in the words spoken by his face, clearly what he said.

Mr. Lee was glad that she herself was not Chinese, today. He was glad that she did not look like she needed to be taken away to the trains. He was glad that she did not look like she could profit from a stay in the place where the train would go. Wherever that was, and whatever it meant. To the landscape at the end of the tracks.

And Mr. Lee was glad that his daughters looked like their mother. That he had not given them on their faces a ticket for the train, had not attached it to them so that they would not lose it, the way one might pin a child's mitten to her jacket. In that way, he was happy not to have been able to provide for them. To have been an unfit father, only in this way. Only today.

The Twenties were over now and things had seemed to be getting better, the Revolution, the Depression: it was all over. But to climb out of something like that a country has to grab a hold of something else, some foothold to lift itself, something to step on. That is what this new decade was for, and that is what the Chinese were for, said the President.

Like Mr. Lee he had said this not in regular words, but with some other part of himself. Something equally understandable, equally forceful.

These kinds of nights happen as one would imagine: the President gets indigestion after a meal of bad fish and spoiled butter, a suspect wheel of cheese. He tries to do something, he tries the carbonating powders.

And more. In pain he orders the arrest of all Chinese in the country and their deportation back to China. Who would complain, after all, or who would complain any louder than anyone else, since there were so many voices of complaint for so many things.

It could have been someone else, the Germans, or people from the United States, the *norteamericanos,* but what was the use. People thought the Chinese were beginning to own everything, and there were just enough of them. In truth, it was that their store signs stood out so much, and their faces. In truth, which everybody knew, there were many other choices, but this one was the quickest.

There were the people in Alamos, for example, who lived next to the great silver mine. The ones who ran the operation, at home they had silver everything, silver broom covers, brooms themselves made of silver, and silver on the pillars holding up their houses. Anything to which silver might be added was fashionable there.

But to get them to give it up, well, that was a different thing.

HIS FOUR DAUGHTERS CRIED when they heard what was happening, and cried when they heard the soldiers getting closer. Jesusita did what she could.

In those days the family lived in Los Apóstoles, twelve row houses, or rather, twelve row rooms, owned by Don Lázaro, who did not worry about things very much, and who when asked said that he most certainly did not rent to the Chinese. With what he charged, he said, one could hardly call it rent.

That there were twelve apartments gave rise to both the humor of the name and the mathematics of a problem. Since they were all built at once and were identical, if one problem arose, there were as if by magic twelve. It was a simple and devastating equation for Don Lázaro, who did not always put much stock in the laws of multiplication.

Through the years, each of these quarters began to take on an individual aspect, as Don Lázaro approached each problem as something different from the one before and the one after. He did not, after all, want to insult anyone by not giving them the consideration of listening to their particular problem. Nor, for that matter, did he wish to offend them by turning down a *café con leche* as he listened. He was a good listener, and sometimes he would offer to boil the milk for the second cup of coffee. And he gave each problem its own solution.

But at the very least, twelve similar-looking yards occupied the space behind these apartments, each with a small fence, or some such barrier. And those who knew their own yard knew their neighbor's.

IT WAS NIGHT BY now, and as the soldiers came and knocked at the first house, Jesusita took her husband into the next yard, and so on down as the soldiers knocked in sequence, as only soldiers with their peculiar efficiency would do.

There were enough garbage cans and compost heaps, enough odd noises by disturbed dogs and grizzled cats, that Jesusita was able to move her husband with some ease. Not the least reason was the irregular rule of geometry, which stated that a small garbage heap was a large mountain to a lazy man. These soldiers were tired already from so much work in the afternoon.

The seven soldiers in the vicinity did not equal one mother calling her child to dinner here. A mother knows how to find a child.

When the soldiers reached the last apartment, Jesusita, who had said she was bringing in laundry, brought her husband back to their rooms, and in through the back door.

His four daughters had said when the soldiers knocked that he was not there, and had not been there for some time, and that they did not know where he was or when he would return, and then shrugged their shoulders.

It figures, said the lieutenant, or the captain, or whatever he was, these Chinese, after all. His voice was a deep voice, and too loud.

The daughters said nothing and went about their business, and at that cue the soldier *harrumphed* and did the same, saying something vague, if you see him, well, you know then, call us, and the daughters replied also with something vague, of course, all right then.

When they left, Jesusita brought her husband in and they all helped to hide him inside the cabinet of the radio, a Ward's "Airline" model, with the word "Heterodyne" underneath. It was a brown piece of furniture, part Greek columns and part lyre in decoration. Before they moved the radio back against the wall, they all looked at him, with the radio tubes and wires all above his head.

He looked like something from the movies, something from a Saturday morning, and they wanted to laugh and cry at the same time. And they heard him say, this cannot be happening. And as they looked at him, they saw that he was right. This was not like doing the laundry or preparing the evening meal. This was nothing they knew. This was after all something from the movies. But it was as if the manager had locked the doors of the theater, and they had to live with this beast.

NO ONE SAW MR. Lee for many years. He did not live here anymore, his family said. But they were not sad. He lived in between the bed sheets and in the bathroom. He fit into the small spaces of the house, and did not eat much.

The soldiers never came back to look for him, but then again there was nothing to look for. Everyone in the town knew that he had disappeared. A pity, they would say, *que lástima.* He was such a smart man.

But times changed, and every now and then people saw him, slowly.

They were not surprised. They understood something of how a thing could happen and not happen. There had been nothing in the newspapers or on the radio about that singular night. They understood how Mr. Lee could be gone and still be here. There was no mystery in seeing something that did not exist. The government had taught them well, and they were good citizens. There were, they knew, many kinds of ghosts.

The rounding up of the Chinese lasted only the one night, as long as the President's heartburn. They loaded them, as people later told each other even in public, into boxcars and open cattle and cotton cars. All over the country the soldiers looked for them, but especially a little farther north, along the border, where they might have been heard by the people on the other side, who might have tried to do something.

Many of the wives who had grown up in this town went with their men, to live in China. They took their children, too, and something or other in their arms. Some of them later came back, and some did not. They were not treated well. But such a thing was not a new life, and they were used to it. Being treated well was not much of a measure for anything anymore.

Not all of the Chinese left, however, and Mr. Lee was not the only one to be hidden. Some men had been dressed like women, and like animals, which was a gypsy trick. And none of them was seen for many years. There was a yipping at the moon some nights during this time, recognizable as coyotes in any other decade, but some townspeople said it was the Chinese. By this they did not mean that they were still in the animal disguises they had worn, but, rather, it was a remark about the quality of voice they heard.

It was a sound reminiscent of the German man, Mr. Luder, whose wife Margarita had died in childbirth along with the child. In the daytime he had a business in clocks, something regular, but every night he slept on the grave of his wife and child, and he wept.

The business later failed, and all he could do was to sleep on that stone and dirt, or walk around the town getting ready to sleep. This walking toward sleep became his job. People, in fact, had sometimes heard Mr. Luder's sobbing, and thought it was coyotes, and later the sounds of the Chinese. It was a sound many animals shared.

Some time later, as many Chinese had made their way up into Arizona, some of them would be mistaken again, this time for Japanese, and taken away once more. They were returned, but again without the courtesy of manners.

When the government later rounded up the Yaqui Indians, they did it the other way around. They could not capture the men. But the women and children who came down from the mountains to trade goods were easy enough to take.

This time they put the women and children in trains, the old trick of how to catch the men, and sent them to the Yucatán just like that. Traveling was dangerous then, as the Yaquis took up the attacking of all the trains in the region, first to try to get their families back and then later out of anger. The Yaquis, many people said, were vicious.

MR. LEE, THE TOWNSPEOPLE remarked regularly, was very smart, but by smart they meant a great deal more, which they could not say. He was rumored not so much to be

Chinese, but to have had a gypsy father himself, who had shown him the ways of other worlds, who had given him the singular ability to live well in a radio. By now they had heard the story of that night from Jesusita. *In our radio,* she said to them, *looking like a Martian.*

Everyone had laughed when Jesusita told the story, but not too hard. Of course, they thought, with a look each to the other. Of course. He was not, after all, of this place.

When Mr. Lee walked along the path between the black walnut trees lining the streets, it was clear now that he had made his place. That the government had not been able to take him, no matter what the law. That he, because of his head that lit up with tubes, knew something more than the law.

They laughed, but not too hard, and they called on him for advice when they were in trouble, because he would understand. They were a little scared of him, of course, because he knew something about things. He knew the underbelly and the tomorrow and yesterday of things, he knew their opposites and their half-turns. He knew the radio, after all, from the inside out.

He was like Mr. Luder, they sometimes said. He knew about life. He knew about it as if he had walked the perimeter of a park, and thereby gauged something of the dimensions of a neat lawn and the heights of the eucalyptus trees.

And Mr. Lee's pronunciation of words, unlike the laws of the Presidents, never changed, a little stilted even after so many years, a little wrong: it showed that he understood their language better than they did, that he spoke correctly. There was something wrong in this place and in these days, and they heard it in Mr. Lee's accent. He would talk, strange-like, and they knew he was right, about anything, about the weather.

The *wedder,* he would say, and they would understand. And when he smoked, they would think they sometimes saw him, some part of him still hiding a little in the cloud.

Spiced Plums

Rosa met José at the circus, and under those circumstances, who would not fall in love? It was the acrobatical amazements, the plantains in sugar, the sure voice of the announcer, the large glass barrels of barley water and rice water, of red teas, the man who spoke the names of these delights loudly as if they were the answer to all questions, *cebada, horchata, jamaica,* and spiced plums, which no one had seen before.

Everything here was what filled the mattress: the stuff upon which to dream, to make love, to sleep. Even to jump, as children do, who have an uncanny sense of knowledge, and know what they are doing, if only with their bodies. To think of the extraordinariness of the circus, and to believe for a moment that a dream and sleep and love are even better, that the circus is only the beginning, that on top of the circus everything is possible.

It was good to think that, even if it were not true. A circus for a mattress, who can explain that to another person? Rosa knew it was better to keep quiet about these things, or suffer the consequences. She would not be laughed at. And for that reason, she never made a movement on her face until she was confident of a thing, in that way insuring that she would not be subject to ridicule.

And indeed and after all, why should she be ridiculed anyway? She did everything correctly, and no one could find fault in that. She was no pair of yellow pants.

José said he could not believe what he was seeing when they met, that she was too perfect, like a picture. Like the circus. The braids of her hair were impeccable, sculpted, almost humming in their tightness, pulling at her scalp in that way that they did. And there it was: she was sculpted, as if out of stone. Not marble, perhaps, but a good stone, solid. Who would not fall in love with perfection, he said later, who.

Rosa when she saw José saw that he smiled at her in a way that no one else had, and that he talked to her with an ease and an immediate intimacy that made her feel he had stepped right in the back door of her house, as if he had only been gone a few minutes and was returning from some trifle, emptying garbage or spading the garden. He talked to her and she felt like the snake in the basket of the circus man who sat on a carpet and played his flute.

She felt herself rise to him, and stay in the sway of his eyes. She could not explain it, only that the song was something inside her that he played, and she heard it even though no one else could. When they walked together after the circus and with her mother's permission, they walked in step. She noticed it, and felt that here was one more part of the song, no matter what anybody else might say.

Something in his manner was a gift, as if it were something real, so that when he laughed she felt she had something to take with her, that when she readied herself for bed she could put it by the night table, and let it stay. And when she did go to sleep that night, she was right. It was there, sometimes as the bark of a dog several houses away, or as the sound of the neighbor leaving his house for his constabulary night job, singular in that it was the only night job in town.

And so on, she thought. She was not given to this kind of frivolous thinking, and it made her nervous.

José of course put everyone at ease, and for that he gathered to himself a small fame. He was everyone's friend, and each thought himself to be on very good terms with him. Wherever José went, he drew a small group, and whenever a newcomer came in, say, to the bar or the café, he would wave that person over and pull up a chair next to himself.

Rosa did not gossip, and so had no knowledge of José other than what José himself told her. And as people knew of Rosa's distaste for passing along information of interest about one or another of the people in town, they let her believe what she wanted. It served her right, they said to each other, when they talked about her.

They loved to see her with José, and they loved to see José with her. She did not know anything of the world, and he thought he knew everything: they were wed in heaven already, according to the laws of magnetism. Heaven, more or less, magnets more or less: everyone thought of those magnets made in the shapes of horseshoes, then of what horseshoes mostly stepped in. And then everyone laughed.

THIS IS HOW IT could have been, how it seemed to the world. That their lives were or would be the circus. That in the making of love everyone suspected the use and overuse of some borrowed device from the circus, a trapeze possibly.

But it was not so.

Nobody could really believe this of Rosa. She was not, as they say, that kind of woman.

It was just that José was exactly just so much that kind of man, how could they not believe it?

Weeks passed, and then months, and when José saw Rosa on Sundays she felt her week-long wait had been sheer madness for him, and that it was all he could bear to keep from lifting her in the air with his arms. Not that she would allow such a thing, of course. But that he wanted to, made her happy inside.

On her mouth it came as a little smile, enough to make him point at it, and act foolish at claiming to detect movement there, stopping passersby and having them look, and then asking for the town photographer. Everyone would laugh, and she would laugh too, since they seemed to be laughing at him.

José was, in fact, happy to see her on Sundays, as he had exhausted himself and everyone else during the week with his stories and his imitations of things. He was glad to see her because he needed someone else to hear what he had to say, to get one more mile out of his tongue for the week.

And by the time she listened to him, he was half tired and half expert already with regard to his stories, and so they came off without too much shine, and without too much crossing of the tongue. They seemed natural to him then, without too much of the monkey, which is what he seemed on Mondays, starting off the week and having to invent a new life each time for himself, with new adventures.

If he had not heard a story for Monday, he made one up, and said that he had heard it, so that one thing led to another and by Friday he was either in trouble or the hero, nothing in between. By Sunday he was resting, and the story seemed like a fine reminiscence, wine-like in its flavor. And she would drink.

Rosa had begun to hope that he would favor her, and come to make the formal first visit that would mean engagement. She was willing, and even more in that he seemed her single prospect in this town and in this life. He took time with her, and never let her leave without making sure of something at least changing on her face. He would study it, and know when he had done his duty, as he called it.

José hoped that no one would marry Rosa, because she was always good for the end of the week. She would listen to him, when no one else would. Not by Sunday.

And so he needed her, and through the weeks dissuaded any talk of anyone showing interest in her. Not that anyone did. He nonetheless threatened to personally kill anyone who would dare to take her from him. Certainly they could borrow her, he said, six days out of seven— but God help the fool who stood in his way on the seventh day. Everyone would laugh, and he would say no, that they must stop. On a Sunday she was the answer to his prayers. They would laugh again, and compliment him on his Catholic devotions.

But he began to believe it, a little, even when he was making people laugh. She was always there to listen to him, these last months, perhaps for this last year entirely. Who could ignore such a thing, he would think, and for all the fun he made of her he saw something in her loyalty to him. If she would agree to a loyalty oath, he began to say, she could be the first in his army.

But in what battle and toward what end? she would say.

His answer was always the same. He would whisper it in her ear, perhaps still something from the circus everyone would say to each other, and she would turn red and say nothing, and thereby say everything. By Sunday and after trying it out so many times, the whispered words always worked.

BUT THE CIRCUS HAD been through town a long time ago. Enough, she thought, of this make-believe.

She decided to trick him in some way, just to get things rolling, though she could not inside herself think of it as a trick, could not imagine such a word like that, absolutely not. It was simply a left-handed stitch instead of a right, she said to herself, and could understand better what she had to do.

And that same week by coincidence, if there is such a condition as coincidence, he would later say—bad luck, of course, but not coincidence—he too decided to trick her, and trick was just the word he used. He wanted her to think he could not see her anymore, since he didn't want her to get any ideas, after all.

He knew about people with ideas, and wanted no part of it. Ideas were his department. And so his task was to find something to fool her but in just the right way, as he was not a callous man after all, and mindful of even the hint of sorrow.

Though who was he kidding, he thought, believing that she cared for him. Still, he did not want to take the chance of his being correct this time. On a card game, yes, but not here.

Her plan was simple, but his plan was simpler.

She would try to get something, and he would try not to get something. Both of their plans were the oldest plans in the world: she would play hard to get, and he would attempt to eat the cake and yet still have it before him as if it had not suffered a single bite.

It was a great plan of the ordinary. She would not come to the park on the next Sunday, so that he would come looking for her, to see if she was ill or if there had been some accident. And if he came, of course, then there it was, plain and simple—a declaration of his love for her, more or less. Or if not his love, at least his commitment to her.

He decided he would not go to the park next Sunday so that she would not see him, and see therefore that he could not be counted upon, no matter what he said. Who knew what he might be up to, and so who would want to know even a single word more about him? She would be tired by him, disappointed, and that would be that.

Which is not what he actually wanted, in truth: in truth he just did not want her to do anything more except be in the park on Sundays to listen to him. But to get that, he figured, he had to go a little farther. It was the way of the world.

THE NEXT SUNDAY NEITHER one of them showed up at the park, true to their separate plans. The day was bright, and the smell of newly-threshed grass filled the air. The boy who sold *paletas* was back, with a double supply of mango and coconut, which were favorites on a Sunday, and spiced plums, which had caught on here after the circus had brought them. On toothpicks, the novelty plums were kept next to the red and yellow tuna cactus pieces, wet with a shared juice. After the summer was over, and for mysterious reasons, no one saw spiced plums again, but everyone remembered.

The cucumber man Serafino was already set up from early morning, throwing his rude peeling knife in the air and almost knocking over the red chile and the cut lemons and the bowl of salt in a daring catch of the large knife by the blade. He certainly did not enjoy catching his knife this way, but doing so was always better than suffering the consequences of an uneventful day's work.

It was his best, if not his favorite, trick, and never failed to draw a small crowd, who said they had better buy now as it seemed he would not last long today. All of them had seen the trick fail more than once, leaving a general scarring on his arms that did not look unlike the red chile and cucumber preparations that he sold.

Rosa, as she was waiting this Sunday in her house, and as she seemed to have nothing better to do, was sent by her mother on a short errand of onions to the *mercado* in spite of her protestations, which she could not fully explain and for which her mother had little patience. Rosa resolved to hurry, and to take the back streets, things she did not do.

Her hurry was that José should not find her outside and think she was going to the park, which would ruin everything, and, equally, she needed to return home soon enough so that if he were to come calling he would find her there, and that would fix everything.

José at this same time was looking for a place to hide, but not looking too well, as he did not want to disappear altogether and miss out on his opportunity to use the last of his stories. But he did not exactly want to be out in the open either, so he decided to go to the house of his friend Lázaro, who always arrived late to the park on Sundays. He would catch Lázaro and his brothers before they left, and keep them with an anecdote he had saved for just such an occasion.

This story was the one about the scorpion and the diaper, which his own mother had only recently told him about his own childhood. Well, it very much explains a great deal about you José, he was sure they would say. The story would be worth the difficulty he had suffered in waiting so long, two whole weeks, to tell it.

Of course Rosa and José ran into each other in the alley behind Huatabampo Street, moving so fast they were upon each other in the time of a finger's snap, and at first they were full of manners, of hemming and hawing to give themselves time to think.

He knows everything there is to know, she thought, just like he said. She could not hide from him even by design. And so, she thought, there it is. She resolved never to hide from him again.

I have been caught, he thought. She must be smarter than he had at first assumed. And her face was so without surprise, without anything to let him know how she had done this. It seemed as if this were nothing, an easy thing for her to have figured out, and he did not feel clever at all. She had taken his cleverness from him in the span of two abrupt seconds.

EACH THOUGHT THE SAME things, that one must pay for deceit. If he tried to get out of this by some joke, thought José, then things would be the same as they were, only Rosa would have an upper hand at having found him out.

And Rosa thought that if she tried to get out of this by telling him she was simply out walking, then nothing would change, and José would think her odd. They resolved in that moment to tell each other the truth.

Not right away, of course, not that very moment. They caught their breaths first, and moved their feet around a little. This kind of thing takes time, they knew, and yet until they told each other everything neither one could leave.

But it was too much time, this idea of telling the truth. Before either of them knew it, and in much the same manner as how they themselves had bumped into each other, there at the far end of the alley was a group of at least fifteen people, who suddenly burst out into laughter and pointed, calling out their names, *José, José, ha,* they said, and *Rosa, Rosa, Rosa.* As if they were children.

These were the solid members of the Sunday park citizenry, who had appointed and collected themselves into a posse for the purpose of seeing why the king and queen of the park had neither one shown up nor sent a proper message to explain their absence.

And of course, aha, they said, *this is just what we thought.* They had already been to Lázaro's house, and look, here is Lázaro himself, who says he has not seen you and does not know of any plans you might have had to come over.

There are no explanations left, José.

Hahh, they said. *We knew it all along, and it's for the best, but you should have told us, there are no secrets here, and why did you take so long, and the kinds of stories you tell, José. We didn't believe this at first. But of course, well here you are, aren't you.*

José and Rosa had each counted on the other one to be in the expected place, and had not for a moment thought about what neither of them being in the park might look like.

Son of a bitch, thought José, which even in thought was almost too much for Rosa to see in his face. *Shh,* she said, as she would say many times to him. As if she could hear what he was thinking, but without understanding it, and again she said *shh.*

You're a bunch of metichis, José yelled to them, *get out of here.* But they had all seen him with Rosa, in this alley. In this town everybody knew what that meant, no matter how much one complained about people being mistaken. It always meant only the one thing.

Rosa knew what was what. His plan was bigger than she had thought, bigger than she had even hoped for: he had used the law of manners and small towns to trap her. And it was all so sudden, she said, as she had heard so many others say.

José's friends had come looking for him, and, out of curiosity, for her too. They found them together, and applauded and whistled. They came to them in the alley, and surrounded them in a ring of hands, allowing them no voice and ignoring their protestations, and in that moment of the inescapable rules of a boy and a girl meeting in a back alley perhaps to kiss and who knew what else the marriage was made. That it was an accidental meeting was not as strong as the plain fact of the two of them caught in front of everybody.

José was not happy and he complained up to the last minute and beyond, but neither was he finally bigger than the law of alleys, which here in this town was everything. No one listened to him in this.

José was a good friend, loyal to those who befriended him. He could not tell them, without them thinking it was a joke like all the other times, that what they had seen was a lie, was not true. He did not like to make dust rise, as they used to say, not like that, not that kind. So he knew they would not believe him. And even if they did, it would not matter, not now.

Joke or not, here was the thing: he had said in the park often enough that he and Rosa were a couple.

And since the circus his friends had seen them to be a couple often enough, even if, José thought to himself, he had only been joking.

Rosa had felt herself to be half of a couple though, and said so, but José had only thought her to be joking, and had said as much himself.

He had not, however, believed it.

But now there was no way out. Here they were, as a couple. Plain as anything, so it had to be true.

To be honest, thought José, there was at least something to be said for the advantage of being the owner of a story like this. It was a mistake, he would say each time for the rest of his life, the whole thing a tragic misunderstanding, an error of epic proportion carrying with it who knew what kind of danger, and his friends would laugh, and pat him on the back. But after all, they said, everybody had seen them in the alley. And here, as they all knew, that was that.

Five

PEOPLE SAID THAT AT night old Don Lázaro the mayor did not simply put his false teeth into a glass of water. No sir, not Don Lázaro. While he was at it, he also unhooked his beard, and put it on the nightstand right next to the water. Then he took off his mouth to give it a rest as well.

With that, he would tuck himself in at night, twice. First, with a fold of the nightstand doily, he tucked in these smaller parts of himself lying on the table. Then, with a regular-business fold of the green blanket on his bed, he covered the rest of his body.

These, everyone said, were Don Lázaro's evening necessities. And every time after saying these things about him, they laughed. That was the thing about Lázaro Luna. There was so much to make fun of. In that way he was like a dessert, and nobody could get enough of him.

The thing about him most of all was that he liked to talk. It was easy to see, then, that when he took out his false teeth at night, he did so not to clean them, but to rest them.

The townspeople further imagined him checking the condition of the dentures' springs rather than the whiteness of the loose teeth. They imagined him wondering, had the springs wrongly allowed him to grind the teeth too far, one against the other, top against bottom? Had he gone the one syllable too many late in the afternoon? Had he talked his own mouth right out of himself?

Knowing him, all of this was certainly possible.

Don Lázaro would also find it necessary, they thought, to check for damage inside the large, pink and black, puckered hole left in his face. This was how they imagined him without teeth, like a bad melon, his mouth an old, loose pink-and-black of worm-like layers upon layers of skin.

Don Lázaro should indeed take care and check. Nobody else was going to do it, that much was certain. Just imagining it was already too much. An opening like that, the townspeople said, it could get clogged up. Then what would he do?

In winter, they hoped he would doubly check: he needed a place especially in that season for the heat steam of his famous beans to come out. Otherwise—well, nobody wanted to say. It was better that they saw this breath coming out of his mouth when he walked in winter. This was the joke of the town.

But it didn't have to be winter. This very escaping steam and smell of boiling Yucatán black beans made, not simply his mouth, but Don Lázaro's whole house on Huatabampo Street look gift-wrapped with ribbons, even in summer. Though it had no numbers, nobody ever mistook his house. It was just like his mouth. The address was simple: he lived next to the five cottonwood trees. Anyone could see them, see the way the steam ropes from his house corralled them into a small herd, the same way his conversation drew people to him, whether they wanted to be there or not.

In all of the stories about him, in all of the town's preoccupation with this man, so much so that he was voted mayor time and again, Don Lázaro was a marvel to the children. They too saw the mist coming from the cracks and windows of his house.

They saw how in winter, when he thought nobody else was looking, he sometimes breathed doubly hard to look himself for this fabled breath of his. He did it forcefully and with laughter, *harrumphing* a little of himself out as spirit into the air, as if he were a child himself again, amused at this trick. For the children who watched him—and all of them did, sooner or later, some in fact becoming experts on the subject—this was enough of a drama, enough of an entertainment for them, a grown man growling out so much whiteness from his face.

Because of these things, and in combination with the hog-calling and netherland noise from the opera records he always played, the children called him dragon-names. They invented a hundred variants, a different name for each day of the cold.

The children of the town followed him, gathering together to say these names, these things to his face, *Lunes Loco, Martes Miedo,* Monday Crazy, Tuesday Scared, in a chant seven or eight times, until finally he would stop them by raising his right arm in a severe gesture.

Old Don Lázaro the Mayor would thereupon pull himself up, look at them with big eyes, then raise his eyebrows as if these themselves were arms being raised as well. The best of military statues did not reproduce the drama of this pose better than Don Lázaro in this moment.

But the children knew to look right back at him, with their hands on their hips, doing their part well in this old game.

Ahhhh! Don Lázaro said, in a growl half dog.

Ahhhh, HAAAAH! the children responded, wolves and bears fiercer than any old dog in their second syllable.

Don Lázaro would have to laugh, and then more smoke would come out of his mouth, and he could not win.

THAT DON LÁZARO TALKED a lot was not the only thing the townspeople said about him. Sometimes on Saturday nights, their own tongues got out and walked around living rooms. From their owners drinking too many beers, these tongues became rude, and were not afraid to say things one way or the other. These tongues danced, too hard sometimes, so that they fell, but even on the ground they did not stop moving, adopting the manner of street dogs taking baths on their backs in the dirt of the alley.

Don Lázaro, these tongues would say. *He should just as well take out his eyes and lie them next to the teeth. He never believes what is plainly right in front of them anyway. He just believes what he wants.*

With Don Lázaro, however, another tongue would say, *it is a point of honor. He respects the rank of his body parts, and does not question them.*

With this, everyone laughed, and contributed to describing the collective half-army of Don Lázaro's body. *Mouth first,* they always said, *general to everything. Well, first or second,* everyone winked, understanding something of Don Lázaro's history in this town. Somewhere far down the list came his eyes, lazy and at the rank of miserable, underfed lieutenants.

The last things on the list were his feet, those poor sub-privates. After all, who could imagine Don Lázaro the mayor actually walking anywhere to back up in person some bit of information or another that his mouth spoke. Certainly not. Feet, and the use of them, belonged to someone else's army.

Even after this discussion of the body part army, they were still not finished with old Don Lázaro. He was, after all, a Saturday night favorite. Especially when he was not there. That is the lot of mayors, and of this mayor in particular.

Finally, they all agreed that if Don Lázaro said something happened, it happened. Then everybody laughed.

This assertion—*If I say it happened, it happened*—had been his signature through the years, stronger and more binding than anything he might have written in ink. *I have said it,* he would say, and that was that. For many years it was in truth a phrase better than any law.

NOT ANYMORE, THOUGH. EVERYONE who knew Don Lázaro, and who knew why it was important to know him, had died. The children of those who knew him, these Saturday night gatherers, knew at best only stories about Don Lázaro. Even these were second or third hand. And they only voted for him as mayor because they thought they had to.

To these young townspeople now, Lázaro Luna looked simply like an old man. Or more carefully said, at least in this town, he looked like the oldest man. The oldest man on earth, as far as anyone could tell. That is what Don Lázaro himself said, anyway.

Since he looked the part to their eyes—eyes being something this new generation believed firmly in using—he was right. Don Lázaro after all had the body and the bearing of a desert tortoise, though he walked with two canes. And always in a suit. That was one of his secrets. To speak loudly, but always in a suit. It had never failed him.

A turtle in a suit these days, however, was a difficult thing. People stood around him when he spoke, which pleased him. But they stood there more to stare than to listen. They knew Don Lázaro's habit of using the mouth first, though the moment might require the eyes or the hands, and his reliance solely on his mouth—where all else was failing—was often an entertainment to them.

Listening to Don Lázaro, and with the perfectly good excuse of his being mayor after all, was a way of getting close enough to get a good look at him without seeming rude. The moment also carried with it the impulse to reach out and touch some part of his skin. Anyone after all would want to know the feel of thousands of years. Or even if he were warm-blooded or cold-blooded after so much time.

Their own eyes gave to them not only the urge to get close, and to touch, but even to bring out a magnifying glass. The moment seemed to carry an element of scientific inquiry. And who is not curious, they said. They did not go so far as to actually touch him, other than to shake hands or to brush against a sleeve. But those who did gather around Don Lázaro always polished and put on their glasses, which they removed immediately for the event from a breast coat-pocket or a purse. He was, after all, something to see.

And their children took photographs, or had themselves photographed next to Don Lázaro when he was not paying attention. They made their move as he directed his concentration and the full reserve of his energy toward gesticulation. Don Lázaro was, after all, invariably pressing the point of some matter of urgency or another, some concern the town *ought to have,* as he would say.

Don Lázaro would ask which kind of salsa, for example, tasted best. Wrapped in the body of a *burro de barbacoa,* which was better? Salsa *casera* or the unspeakable other kind? He did not require an actual answer.

To get Don Lázaro really going, however, one brought up black beans. This was an event to savor. People knew not to bring up black beans unless they had an afternoon free, and a camera. The whole affair took about an hour. Of course it could take a great deal longer, if one tried to actually enter the conversation.

But it was a good hour. That was the bonus. The photogenic hand movements and different looks on his face were eloquent curiosities and conversational horseback rides, even after so many years. These were photographs worth something. They were easy to point at and hold. From Don Lázaro's presence in them, one understood something of the reasons for inventing photography in the first place.

Children through the years kept bringing one or another photo of Don Lázaro to school. They showed the photographs around during the lunch hour, or disrupted class by passing them as if they were love notes. Finally, at least one sixth-grade teacher in an act of inspiration made the photos required study.

"Who would not want to invent photography?" said the teacher. "Who would not want to keep a face like that, with the eyes in such a position, for all time? Was this not also the reason for going to the theater? Or the impulse toward art?"

The teacher tried hard, and the children laughed hard. Then the teacher herself laughed hard. But it was true, and they saw it.

This was the children's Don Lázaro. The Saturday night adults told things a different way, or remembered other details. One fiesta day morning, they would say, a *dieciseis de septiembre* in 1952 ... Even at the simple start of the story, there was already laughter. Everybody knew what was coming.

Nonetheless, they did not stop telling what happened. On this day he was having a particularly energetic discussion about black beans with no one in particular. But because of his furiously waving arms, saying this and that to the air, he changed the entire direction and tempo of the drum and bugle corps, passing at that strategic moment as part of the morning's parade.

Some unfortunate buglers mistook his hand movement as an urgent sign. Because of its sharpness, they thought the motion was a message passed along from the front, from the conductor, saying to pick up the pace of things. So they did.

Nine bugles then hit against the ten or twelve heads in front of them. Heads moved forward in sequence all through the parade. A child watching the whole spectacle at that moment sideways, lying in the arms of his mother, would remember this instant many years later. He would see a white cue ball in a game of billiards. He would laugh, lining it up and hitting it against the perfect formation of the rest.

ON A MORNING YEARS after that particular parade, Don Lázaro emerged from his house. The structure was not much of a house any longer, as not even its famous steam came out of the cracks now. The house was old, and it needed the steam to stay inside, to hold everything up.

It was ten in the morning, as was usual for his walk. He wore the first of his two suits and a hat for the sun.

Of late he had grown a close-cropped white beard, as shaving had begun to take its toll on his face. To unfold his folded face, and then to shave usefully, had been taking almost his whole morning. He had begun to forget breakfast, as the work took him toward lunchtime.

The beard was better, but Don Lázaro then began spending as much of his mornings now with the trimming as with the earlier shaving. The resulting growth was so perfectly drawn, however, that it looked false. This is what later caused the joke of his unhooking it off his face at night, along with his mouth. Underneath the perfect beard, his mouth looked perfect as well, more perfect than it used to. It seemed to get smaller as the beard grew bigger, and this was cause for comment.

Nobody said that Don Lázaro trimmed the skin of his mouth, of course. Who had heard of such a thing? Then again, neither would this surprise anyone. His mouth did look smaller after all. And when Don Lázaro started something, he did not stop until he thought it done.

ON THIS MORNING DON Lázaro walked a little faster than usual. Not much, but a little, which amounted to a great deal for him. Don Lázaro had taken as his morning's mission the delivery of his mayoral and ancient presence to the home of Consuelo Martínez de Calderón, who was expecting a child at any moment.

This in the main was his job as mayor these days, and he did it faithfully. Added to this, he had known the woman's mother, Rosa. He had known her well, the wife of his best friend, and so it was something he wanted to do. It was his way to remember them all young, by seeing this woman, who had all their faces.

Chelo—he knew her most by her childhood name— this woman, Consuelo, and her family lived a small distance over from him, on Obregón Street. Theirs was the house painted green. It was made even more green by the healthy hedge and the big, painted altar to Saint Anthony in the front yard.

With so much green, after a while people began dropping other green things into the yard. There was something about this town and the making of things their own. There had been the story many years ago of the great gardens of Lamberto Diaz, to which everyone had contributed, so that the gardens did indeed become great expanses, big in the town's history, big in its stories.

This time around, and this time in the Calderóns' yard—Chelo's yard—there were first a few smaller statues, a frog and a cactus. Then a piece of plastic fruit, which was per- haps an avocado. A year after the Calderóns had painted the house green and put in the hedge, it was now a showplace of greens. Mr. Calderón tried cleaning up several times, but it didn't work. The green things all found their way back.

That's what happens when there's too much of something, Don Lázaro would say, it makes even more. No- body argued with him. He was talking about the green, but everyone who was listening thought of Don Lázaro's capacity for speech.

As was the custom of the town in these days, Don Lázaro had been more or less invited to make his birth pronouncement. People said that a baby could not be born if the parents did not okay the birth with him. Nobody knew why, but they thought of it as the law. And it was the law, in the way that these things in a small town work.

Don Lázaro would come by and look things over. He would walk around the house grimacing. He would hold his breath for a minute, and those gathered in the house would hold their breath too. Then he would smile. He would say loudly that the baby could be born *because I have said so.*

Then he would stay for lunch.

The town was much bigger now, and there were so many children, this had become his job. The town, it could take care of itself, he would say. But babies, they need help.

As he had begun to forget breakfast, because of so much work he often had no time for dinner either. These lunches were, the townspeople came to say, the only thing now that kept Don Lázaro from disappearing.

He had after all in these last years grown exceedingly thin. Some people suspected he no longer had any body at all. Perhaps, they began to say on Saturday nights, Don Lázaro's suit was still on hangers.

Perhaps he then threaded these hangers cleverly under his beard and hung them up over his ears. This would allow the suit to drape down and give the appearance of a man. In this way, Don Lázaro could remain at his leisure, not worrying about getting dressed while at the same time still letting his suit hang inside his closet. In his closet and in front of them at the same time, just like that.

If this were true, unhooking his beard at night also would mean unhooking and putting his suit away. That would leave him without a body. Don Lázaro only had a face-size shaving mirror in his house, after all, and he devoted its use entirely to his face. Perhaps he had not noticed the gradual disappearance of his body.

It was all right, though, they said. This meant that at night he only wrinkled the pillow and not the sheets, and his housekeeping was surely much easier that way.

HE WAS THIN, THEY knew, but he remained strong. Nobody argued that. He handled his two canes as if they were part of him. Two or three canes. There was, of course, this story of the third cane with which he walked, the one he kept between the others. That appendage was still there, if only because it had been so big—if not physically, then by story. So often talked about, his third cane had grown larger and stronger in people's minds, until they imagined he was like the car that advertised itself as having three headlights.

People said that everybody in this town was related to Don Lázaro. Three headlights was right, and he had shined on everybody. They said that this was why everybody had to take such care with him. In some fashion or other, he was everybody's uncle. Uncle or more, it was difficult to say— everybody having what looked like his black hair after all.

Lázaro knew what they said. It was not finally a sexual appendage at all that helped him walk. He would just wink, and let it seem to be. But Lázaro knew this thing about which the people talked was all just talk.

What Don Lázaro had down there, now and always, even when he was young and the talk made more sense, was an extension of the spine. It was not what people thought. It was something else, something not given to reproductive capacity at all. Here was the trick of the old and the young Lázaro Luna.

Here was an appendage that was hard and thick, all right, just like the stories about him. It was his manhood all right. But this appendage pointed downward, with a permanence in that direction. It was strong because of sadness now. It was as if because of sadnesses in life he had with fierceness determined that he should not fit with a woman. Or else he was simply this stubborn not to marry.

In this way he did walk with three canes, but it was not what people grinned about. He was indeed as they thought everyone's uncle, but only that. This was Don Lázaro. Being related to the whole town in one way or another was his happiness and his sadness both. It made him feel good to have the sadness of his insides looking like a happiness of outsides. And this feeling did look like a something, all right, in his pants.

Whatever he imagined, and whatever the people imagined, it was his life. All of those imaginations together made him strong, whether he was or not. But the strength of that third cane in his pants was not from having women— well, not more than a meager share. It was because in his life he had been too nice after all for his own good. He was related to everyone, all right, but most often from simply helping. In his life he had loved his women too much. What these women made big were his eyes and his heart. In this way, he was married to everyone.

His gift to the women he had known, and therefore to their families, and to their husbands, and to their children thereafter, was the saying of nothing to the rest of the world.

His gift was to hold them, but not where people thought. And they held him tightly as well.

THIS MORNING ON THE way to Mrs. Calderón's house, Don Lázaro was late and hurrying. He was already thinking about the afternoon. It was his habit to spend afternoons indoors, at the Molino Rojo. He liked to spend his time with the men closest to his age, the ones he had known as children. In the Molino Rojo they were all children again.

Don Lázaro played dominoes and *lotería* with them, sometimes a card game from the last century. Something they all remembered. He no longer drank the beer, but an amber beef broth, which looked close enough. At some time over the years the owner of the bar, Don Misterio, or Missy as he was called inside this place, had changed Lázaro over from the beer to the broth. Lázaro had seemed not to notice. In these later years, Missy had also taken to warming it for him.

It was that broth which was on his mind today. *What a drunkard!* he thought to himself because he wanted the drink so much. He tried to forget. He *harrumphed* his throat. He grizzled his face by moving his mouth upward toward his nose, then from left to right. He stopped to balance himself on his canes and adjust his hat.

That hat had served him well through the years, like his suits. It covered what was no longer there, but what he remembered. It covered so many years of black hair. He wore the hat all the time, he said, to those who would still listen, because it kept the sun off. What Lázaro really thought was that sometimes the hat seemed to keep him from climbing out of himself with his old strong arms.

The hat blocked the top of his head, stopped it from opening like a hatch whose hinges were under his eyebrows. Without the hat, the hardness and the heaviness of the hat, sometimes Lázaro could feel something inside himself. He could feel what it wanted to do. It was the real himself in there. It was just waiting with his old strong arms to get a little hold on the outside world. It wanted to come up as if from a rabbit hole, one hand on each side of his head, coming out through his ears. He imagined then a pulling of himself up, and crouching on his elbows. Then the rest of his old self would come up, the way he remembered himself to have been. Young.

Lázaro could hear himself inside his body some days, grumbling at this long wait. Everything inside himself was strong and wanted to catch up with where he was going, to run faster and farther and past all his friends, the way he always had done, to just get moving. In there, inside, he wanted that run, to stretch his young legs again and take a big breath. He wanted to pump those arms, and run.

AS HE WALKED BRISKLY, as briskly as he could, along the street, Don Lázaro adjusted his hat carefully with both hands until it was tight and he could feel it. He looked up momentarily, as was his habit, at his fingers as they adjusted the brim.

He looked up, as he had done a thousand times. By chance his hands in this position shaded his eyes so that he could see clearly upward into the sky, whether he wanted to or not.

Up there, up in the sky, he saw a five. A cloud *five,* the numeral, clearly shaped. 5.

He blinked his eyes, which no wonder he had never trusted. What people said was true. He trusted his mouth. He knew good food when it entered, and he knew good words when they exited. That was that.

But these eyes, with their half-silver and their milky excesses, they were up to their old business.

He blinked his eyes again, and thought he was right never to have trusted them. *What is a five doing up there?* he said to himself. *Why not a nine? Why not an angel, a vision in which one might believe?* But it was a five.

Seeing something first and then being forced to make something of it went against Don Lázaro's grain. He always had the answer first, and then, if necessary, he found the problem.

He had to think fast. Perhaps it was the circus. He was about to say, *the damn circus,* but he stopped. He would not have meant it. He had too much love, too much history with circuses. He was in awe of the men who drove motorcycles in the huge, metal-mesh cage, around and around. They drove themselves upside down and even seemingly against each other and against gravity and against Nature without ever colliding.

Maybe a troop of white birds from the circus, thought Lázaro. Perhaps this was the newest of their marvels, a troop of white birds trained to make fives. A good trick.

He let that thought work inside himself for a minute. But on the outside, the hinges of his eyebrows began to make too much noise, demanding his attention again.

No. After all, what kind of white birds capable of making fives would come back down to the circus? No. They could get a job anywhere.

Nothing more was left to think. The boys at the Molino Rojo would have a good laugh about this one. God's joke, he would go in there and say. God, just to see if we are on our toes down here. Just to see if we are gullible enough to make something of a ridiculous big five in the sky. Ha. As if it were a recipe for cheese or, better, something new about beans, something useful.

UPON DON LÁZARO'S ARRIVAL at the house of Consuelo Calderón, the cloudy essence of the five had caused its bold lines to deteriorate. It had by now become a weak version of its former numerical self, hardly worth pointing at. It left only a dragon-like set of wisps, an any-old-rag of a cloud.

Don Lázaro averted his eyes and brought them to their regular business of being the silent and secondary partners to his mouth. He knocked on the Calderón door and announced himself without even a half-look up once more.

Don Lázaro was immediately welcomed into the full house. The men did not slap him on the back exactly, but had one seen the action in silhouette one would have thought so. They were careful with him, not quite willing to see what would happen to Uncle Lázaro should he truly be welcomed like a young man to the house.

There were no instructions for men like Don Lázaro anymore. No good directions existed on how to put them back together. Already some of his parts were missing. And some got added that did not belong, but which were the only ones available to do a job. Though he had the fine suit, for example, this last winter he could find no decent vest. He wore a reasonable section of tablecloth in its place. It did not match precisely, but it did the job. In fact, it did the job of the vest and of a napkin, both at the same time, so that it was perhaps even better than what had been.

And given the tortoise quality of Don Lázaro's skin, so many folds and bends, one of his elbows had been replaced by a near-sighted toad. One could make it out bulging a little under his sleeve after he removed his coat. If Don Lázaro bent his arm there, it made a noise. It may not in fact have been an actual toad under his coat sleeve. It might have been something worse.

Some said the protrusion was, instead, from too many years at the Molino Rojo. They said it came from too many hours of his elbow on the bar, and that it was not a real toad at all. Others said that, in point of fact, a weak-eyed toad had simply followed Don Lázaro home one day, and he had not noticed.

Given the fussing noise of this toad, nobody could say that there was not even perhaps an assemblage of other animals under his suit, some congregation of the small wild. They had all heard the other noises after all. They knew the growls and small barks when he sat at his leisure on the couch. They looked at each other when he rose. They could hear an occasional whinny as if from a very small horse, something not more than an inch or two in height somewhere in this man. This was not simply an elbow they were talking about.

DON LÁZARO WAS TAKEN immediately to the bedside in question. Mrs. Martínez de Calderón here in this bed was just Chelo to Lázaro again. Young and with a slight shining through it all, she gave him a smile, which he returned. In that exchange, and with a woman, he was still very much the man he had been.

For a moment, it was the Don Lázaro of memory. For a moment, between the two of them in that room, it was two smiles by themselves, two lines disembodied in space, floating on the lines of a good lake, in summer and to the breeze.

The doctor had made no particular fuss, and there was no history in the family to prepare anyone for what Don Lázaro was about to say. His mouth had come prepared, not with questions but with answers, again.

Don Lázaro *harrumphed* his throat and grizzled his face, so that the room could ready itself. He held his breath. They held their breath.

Then he said, "You will have five children today."

Everyone looked at everyone else, and then at the floor. They tried not to laugh.

"I have said so."

"Well then," said Chelo, who took Don Lázaro's hand in her own, "we will name four of the five after you." The two of them smiled again at each other, and he nodded his head in a *yes*.

Neighbors, who had come to help, served Don Lázaro and the others lunch. They made black beans specially, to let Don Lázaro talk. Then they all joked about one thing or another.

Theirs was a good lunch, said Don Lázaro. He meant it. After finishing, he slept awhile, then excused himself and said his good-byes.

Don Lázaro walked off toward the Molino Rojo. He walked as a zoo of a man, his toad, his three canes, himself when he was young, his mouth with the life of its own. This bursting man who would not burst walked down the street and turned left.

Though they referred to it as a *Six,* the newspaper the next day explained Don Lázaro's Five-cloud in the sky. It had been the failed attempt of an itinerant skywriter. The idea of writing in the sky with smoke from an airplane was popular that year, but untested. There the sky was, as if it were a big blank of paper no one had thought to use.

The man in the airplane had been trying to paint "Pepsi-cola" in the sky. It was an immodest effort to bolster sales and compete with the more popular Coca-cola.

It didn't work. The pilot had only been able to generate enough smoke to print the first letter, *P.* Even then, because he knew right away things were not going well and became nervous, the pilot printed the *P* upside down and backward in its fancy script.

As Don Lázaro walked along, and into the Molino Rojo, for the first time his mouth failed him. He had so much to say, but there was nothing to talk about. While this had never stopped him before, all he could talk about now was what everyone else talked about. The five stayed in his eyes. Who would have thought this, he thought to himself. Who would have thought this, after so many years. The one thing he wanted to say did not after all live in the big house of his mouth.

Susto

THE WHOLE AFFAIR WAS not much: the neighbor boy Noé had come over the vine-covered white wall, he made no noise, and he so positioned himself that he might watch to his heart's fill Mariquita hang the laundry. But Noé could not stand quietly.

Halfway between her bending and her lifting, Mariquita heard something. She at first thought the sound to be the movement of crickets or of sparrows, and then of rabbits. But it was the boy Noé, who could no longer hide. He showed himself to her as the noise she had heard. He stood with his hands to his side and his mouth half open or, as they say, half closed.

In truth Noé's mouth was neither half open nor half closed. His mouth held to a point of openness from which, after this moment of the world standing still, all other uses of his mouth would be measured. His mouth would always be either wider or narrower than this point at which he stood there looking at her, and she at him.

Noé would measure the rest of himself also in this manner, against how he stood here looking at her. When he would turn his body from that day thereafter, his arm would be closer or farther away from where it hung as he faced her. When he would bow his head, it would be farther down from the position it held at this long second that now defined him.

Noé said nothing, and for an instant neither could this girl Mariquita make sense of the moment. She kept steady the position she had held when he saw her from the wall. She stayed stooped over as if continuing to pick up something wet made of cotton in the heap that filled her yellow basket.

Mariquita bent and then she unbent herself. She collected the clothing around her. Then the use of her ears, which from surprise had closed themselves, came back. In her hand she could feel the moisture from having been holding the wet laundry. Then her voice came back. It let loose at first the same sound she had heard at the start of this long moment. Like that first noise, it too made a sound stolen from the movement of crickets, or of sparrows. Her voice came out as a chirp or a swallowing. The noise grew then into the round, fuller noise of rabbits in a thicket of vine.

It was a shout, and then it was a scream. As a scream the noise of her voice was thinner, and faster. It moved into, and then along, the ribs and wisps of breeze.

Mariquita was not afraid. She was surprised, but it was surprise from the left side of things. Yet, it was not funny. It was not delight. It was instead the surprise that comes before fear. Being scared follows like a mother to the rescue of her naive child. But it takes a second. The mother is physically able to be there only as quickly as her body can run.

So Mariquita was surprised, at first. But then as soon as she could be, she was afraid. It was the mother in her coming from the back of her head to the front. It was a second late, but there as fast as it could, taking care. This was the screaming now.

Noé stood immobile, as if the noise had been a light shined in the face of a wild animal at night. He stood hypnotized, and could not hear, as if his own ears did him no service. He stood and used only his eyes, which were big. They saw only this girl's mouth, which was open. *Hello Noé,* her mouth seemed to say, *welcome,* and *come here.* His eyes saw her arms lift, as if to embrace him. He saw those arms rise, as if to say where had he been, and why had he taken so long, so many years to arrive?

Mariquita stopped her scream, because she had no more breath. She saw him and then was sorry, and not sorry. She embarrassed herself making so much noise. But she was embarrassed too that he stood there. Like the boy Noé in that moment, the embarrassment and the noise both so big, Mariquita could still not move.

At that, the neighbor boy Noé did move. He came to her, because she did not run like a rabbit. Though he had waited, she did not fly off like a bird. He knew her capable and thought her ready to lift herself into the air. He expected her every second to move away from him and from the earth, taking everything from his own insides with her.

Noé expected to see her flying, that he would see her waving her arms to sustain herself up in the air, above the houses and against the horizon. He expected to try following her, to find her in the branches of the walnut trees at the edge of town. He imagined climbing the trunk of the tallest tree, to try coaxing her toward his hand. He fully expected her, however, to fly again, and that he would lose her once more to the sky.

All of this in a passing of seconds. But when Mariquita screamed, her true mother came immediately running from the kitchen. Her brother jumped from the side-house, with tools in his hand, a drill and a ruler.

Then a neighbor from the other side lifted himself over the wall. Someone who had been passing the front of the house came running to the side gate, and opened it.

The small dog that had been cooling itself under the foundation of the house came with his teeth barely in his mouth.

They all came to see in that moment the neighbor boy Noé with his arms around Mariquita, giving her his kind of kiss, which was some other offering. It was something not quite, something from the attempt and the finish of a kiss both. But it was not the thing itself, for which he was either too shy, or had no real knowledge. This kind of kiss was something given from the moisture of his mouth to the strong side of her neck.

Mariquita also had her arms raised. However, she raised her arms not around him, but in front of him. She raised them against the middle of Noé's embrace, the elbows of her arms at his ears. They could not hear anything because of how hard her arms were covering them.

All Noé knew and all that mattered was that he had caught this Mariquita before she flew. So she must care for him after all, he thought. After all, so often had he walked past the house. So many times had he walked past her on Sundays. So many times had they passed at the *verbenas* for the rain on the *Día de San Juan,* and at the day-markets.

Noé could not have hoped for anything more than this in the world. He had left so many gifts on the top of the wall, combs and colored rocks, feathers and gingerbread *cochitos.* He had hoped for just this. She could not move. By not moving she must therefore understand why Noé himself also could not move. He believed then that she had after all received his gifts with grace. He was finally welcome. That she could not move meant *yes*.

MARIQUITA'S BROTHER HIT NOÉ in the small of the back with the curved wood and steel of the drill he was carrying. Mariquita's mother took up the scream that her daughter had begun, and carried it to safety, wanting to take even that away from this boy. It was as if the scream were some bodily part of Mariquita. And this part, like a rabbit, was jumping out of her body into the arms of her mother, who had reached the back step of the house.

The man who had been passing took Noé by the arms from behind, and the neighbor pushed against Noé's side with his shoulders.

But it did not take so much. The force of their efforts, so much pull backward and pushing sideways, toppled all of them over onto the grass. Noé could smell the quality of straw in this yellowed grass suddenly broken, as he lay there with his face pressed into it by an elbow against the head.

With his head kept still like that, and his eyes from the force made even larger than they already were, he could see Mariquita in the arms of her brother. He held her the way Noé himself would have liked. But Noé was content, and made no struggle. He was pleased to be at least close to what he wanted.

As her mother had taken over the scream, Mariquita, with her second breath, returned to surprise and did not think she was afraid any longer. The incident seemed suddenly like nothing now, and to hold Noé down like that was too much.

It was nothing, Mariquita said. She looked at this boy Noé, trying to recognize his face.

Mariquita's mother came and took over, nodding with her head at the men to let this boy get up. The neighbor pulled Noé upward by the arm, and held it too high to be comfortable. Noé looked down now, away from Mariquita. He could not look at her in front of all these people, not the way he wanted. And he did not want Mariquita to see him looking at her any other way.

In the look that had passed for a second between them, before all of this noise, before anyone else had seen the two of them, each unable to move, holding and not holding each other, Mariquita many years later would recognize an act of confession. That he now looked down at the ground said nothing, though the people who gathered said that it meant he was sorry.

This boy Noé was not sorry, she knew, or sad. He did not mean to scare her. But she could tell he was not sorry that he had awakened this morning, come to the wall, and jumped over. In his big eyes Mariquita could see, *what is there for which to be sorry?*

In those eyes Mariquita could see a long way. They were inhumanly big, as if she could fit into them, as if her arms could reach right in, all the way up inside him. As if she could take what was there, and lift it right out. She saw him in this full way, but nobody else did. In the space of the split second, she saw him as much as he saw her.

But it was too late to stop herself, to stop her voice and her body. Because she screamed he must have hurt her, they said.

Did he hurt you? would have been something she could answer. Instead, they asked her, *where did he hurt you?* They looked at her also with their eyes. But their stares were different from the way Noé had looked at her. She could not reach her arms into these people. These people felt to her like the opposite of Noé. They did not make room inside themselves. Their eyes seemed instead to be trying to get into her, making even more of a crowd there than she already felt.

There was nothing, she said. *He, well he grabbed me, but there are no bruises. I don't feel anything.*

The bruises have not yet come up, they said. They looked at her arms and neck, and waited with certainty, nodding their heads at each other. *These kinds of bruises will be yellow at first. Then they'll get worse.*

But he didn't hurt me, Mariquita said.

Then you would not have screamed, of course. You cannot know, in a state like this. You will see. This kind of boy. He is an animal. Just look at him.

Noé did not raise his eyes or his head. They dragged him, because he could not walk for them, through the side gate to the front yard to wait for the police.

Mariquita saw only Noé's back, which had already begun to grow huge, gathering into itself the disproportionate misfortunes of his life. She realized she knew this boy more by his back than his face. He had always taken his face too quickly past her. Mariquita knew him well from this back. She watched it fall now, the same way it had fallen each time he had passed by her, thinking then she was no longer looking in his direction. But each of those times she had continued to watch him. He was a curiosity after all, looking like he did, this sway-back horse boy.

IN THE MONTHS BEFORE this wrestling of Noé to the ground, Mariquita had been finding things. She took the comb from on top of the backyard wall and carried it to her mother. It had shined in the sun, and Mariquita had at first thought this comb to be a bird perched there at some small business of insects. But the bird was a comb, and in remarkable condition for having been on the wall for who knew how long.

How would a comb get lost on a wall, wondered her mother. It made no sense to either of them. *Some tricky-business at work,* said her mother, who tucked these words away under her apron for later. She said the words not so much for Mariquita to hear, but so she would remember them to tell her husband. *Some kind of tricky-business,* she said again quietly, and clucked her tongue.

Mariquita said nothing, and the next day came back from the wall with a piece of blue paper cut and folded into the shape of an elephant. She did not bother to show it to her mother this time. It was only a piece of paper, after all, not worth anything. But it was in the same place as the comb.

Then she found a fir cone, though this was not a landscape of pine trees. She did not know what it was, and so, simply to get an answer, asked her mother what it was.

Where did you get such a thing? her mother asked, and after Mariquita answered, her mother repeated the answer, but as a question: *in the same place again? You found this where the comb was? How can that be?* Mariquita shrugged her shoulders.

It's funny-business, her mother said. *Don't you go back over there until I tell your father.*

With that, Mariquita thought nothing more about the objects. They were, after all, funny-business, whatever that was. And she liked them.

Two days later, here came the neighbor boy Noé, who might himself have been a pinecone had anyone looked at him from the inside out.

This boy took her shoulders with violence, and left bruises. We saw it all. He shook her, and tried to carry her off. It was a good thing we were prepared. We knew there was funny-business, we all said so, but who would have guessed, a boy like this, an animal.

He should be shot, said Mariquita's father. He added with authority that they could count on him for the job.

The police took Noé from the yard. When they put him in jail they gave him a kick to the leg for his own good, which sent him onto the floor. He stayed there on the floor, but for too long. This scared the deputy, who finally helped Noé onto the bed and gave him some water.

After a great deal of noise and argument between Mariquita's father and the captain in the outside office, no charges were finally made. No one knew what to do with Noé. The captain did not want him in the jail, not without a family who could pay for his release. And Mariquita's father, when it got down to business, preferred that any shooting be done by the captain. They agreed only that Noé was not fit even for keeping in a jail.

Noé heard nothing. After Mariquita's father left, and they were certain he was no longer in sight, the police finally let Noé out. They sent him home without explanation, the deputy hitting the side of Noé's head with the flat of his hand. *What do you think about that,* the deputy said, and with his chin pointed Noé out the door.

Noé did not go home. Instead, he followed without stopping the direction of the man's chin until he could not any longer. He had listened to that chin too hard, or had not listened at all. In any event, Noé ended up walking out the door and on in that straight line for five days until he fell.

After walking so far, Noé never was quite able to move quickly again. The earth where he fell attached itself to him, so that he became odd-shaped, heavy at some angles and thin at others. He had slow bones, they would say in the new towns, and it was true.

People heard about Noé living in various places thereafter, and they nodded their heads. His family, when they nodded their own heads upon hearing the same bits of news—that it was a cave he lived in, or a stall among sheep, even a house that was a railroad car—let out a deep breath as well. At least he was somewhere, and maybe these places were not so bad. What was there to do? they would say. The person to whom they were speaking would also give a nod of the head.

AFTER A FEW DAYS, when the fussing had finished and the boy Noé could not be found, Mariquita went back to her chores. She did not worry. They all kept an eye on her, and took care to pay attention when she was in the large backyard.

Nobody believed anything more could happen. Such a thing, they all agreed, occurs only once. The boy was gone at any rate. Still, they were prepared should he by some quirk come over the wall again.

The boy Noé had been invisible when he had lived in this town, and then suddenly when he was gone he was everywhere. Mariquita did not understand it.

She had said she was not hurt, but her family knew what was what. She had the *susto,* they said—she had been given *the scare.* They could see this illness in the circles under her eyes and in the way she dropped things and was irritable.

Though she protested, they took her to the *curandero,* who made his cure of brown chicken eggs and vinegar. He made her come back again several times throughout the night to stand with the moon. This recommendation was not dissimilar from his remedy for the other diseases with which he was specially charged in curing, the *empache* and the *caída de la mollera,* those diseases for which regular doctors had no name, this blockage of the intestines or the sinking in of the crown of the head.

It had been the *curandero's* luck and his fate to be born a twin, which was the equivalent in these matters of a diploma. At least, thought Mariquita, she did not have the *caída.* He did not have to put his fingers into her mouth and push on the roof to make the head come back to its roundness. At least that, she thought.

So many words, so much whispered noise, and the noise itself rising as if it were smoke. This was the cure.

The moon appeared to her as if it were one more piece of cotton from the field. It looked as if it would to itself take in from her what was wrong, in the way that one dabs something from the skin. This was the simplest cure of things, just to wipe them away. Hers, she thought, was such a small event, and she said as much. But in need, the *curandero* said, of the entire moon for its cure. *The small things,* he said, *this is how they are.*

These matters take time, said the *curandero* of his methods, *but they work, without a doubt.*

He said his words with force, so who could not believe him? Anyway, his fees were reasonable. The night did not cost much, thought Mariquita. This made her feel better for everybody.

Mariquita paid it all little attention, and did what this man asked. To see her do odd things in the night made her family and the *curandero* happy.

And the cure was, in truth, a cure. Mariquita after a while did not think about the boy Noé any longer. She did not recall his name. Then again, not much had happened in that backyard with that boy, and so there was not much to remember.

However, she did not feel her recovery to be quite the miracle her parents did. They nodded their heads in approval to each other when she walked through any room in which they happened to be seated. They made the simple act of walking seem as if it were all the cure anyone would need for anything in this world. Mariquita thought, perhaps they were right. Still, just walking was just walking.

The objects from the wall, not all of which she had told her mother about, she discarded, for the most part. The comb she kept for a few years as it was a perfectly useful comb.

One morning, early, when there was no light in the room yet, Mariquita grasped for a glass of water on the night table. In doing so she knocked the comb from the bureau to the floor. In her effort to rise from the bed to see what had fallen, Mariquita stepped on the comb with her bare foot. The foot hurt a little at the snap, so that she held it in her hand and sat back down to feel if there was blood.

But there was none. It simply felt like she had cut herself. She checked again, because she had been certain, but nothing. She did everything twice in these days, and everything she did was small. She had begun to feel this smallness of her world, even if she had forgotten its name.

Everything in fact was small now in comparison to the walls and the ceiling of the living room that had been in Noé's eyes. Those eyes were his true house. This was what she did remember, if not his name. They were the place in which he lived.

His eyes were a shelter for Mariquita as well. In them was what he had wanted to give her in the moment he had looked at her in that backyard, looked at her so hard. It was a half-second century in which he had seen for them both the possibility of their lives as husband and wife together. It was as if he took his two eyes and made them one, like binoculars, bringing their two lives closer and into focus. Mariquita had seen it all, but not only with eyes.

She did not remember Noé's name, and she did not remember very much about him. This much was true.

But that half-second, which she did remember, made her large inside, made her feel awkward and fat, made her bump into things. This comb she knocked over now, it was not the first time. And she knocked the comb over not with her hand, but with what was inside her hand.

And her foot did in fact bleed, but it was not blood exactly. It was something from inside her blood.

What Mariquita did remember from the backyard was Noé inside her. She remembered how the two of them together in her small skin could not fit.

Not Like Us

His laugh was like rabbit droppings, each separate gatling sound small, high-pitched, not much of anything. But added up together into his version of a laugh, these spitted sounds were suddenly a gang, menacing by virtue of their numbers. These noises connected like pearls on a string but without their shine, or Chinese firecrackers, too close. Too ready to explode. When one burst out, the rest could only follow.

His was a laugh, but only if he said so.

The desk clerk was clear on this point, and waited for instruction obediently.

The visitor stood there waiting for information on his room, but not for long. When the clerk did not respond, the man reached over and took a key from the shelf.

Well, he said, *I can see if a man wants to get any sleep around here, he's got to do it himself.*

THE JOURNALS OF COLUMBUS recount mermaids in the New World, said Mr. Lee. The sailors called them *Sirenas,* and implicit in that notation was the existence of the *Tritones,* their husbands, though not one of them was ever actually spotted. They were more of a Saturday evening guess.

Perhaps, the townspeople said, the *Tritones* were simply too lazy to show themselves, or so terrible that nobody who saw one ever survived. No good either way.

The journals recount the mermaids singing as God's own daughters at night. Of course, we think now, common sense, said Mr. Lee, this singing at night. Who sings their best songs in daylight, without a dark stage from which to emerge, without artificial, and therefore special, footlights? Who hands over a tip in the daytime, where everyone can see? The *Sirenas* sing their songs only at night. They sing when the world is halfway toward the show of dream, when reaching into the pocket for a coin is a reach down into sleep and what resides there by way of desire.

At sea, anyway, no one sings in the daytime. Not for show. There is work to be done in the daylight, whatever work it is that sailors do, trim the sails, avast the hearties.

But when the sun sets, the accordions come out. The tattooed sailors smile their fish-like grins, full of sea meat and eel tongue and North wind. They start the push and pull of their musical boxes. They dance in their striped shirts and, slyly so that the other sailors do not see, retie their bandannas against the air, which has begun to cool. We imagine them half reasonable men who get cold, half something from the old movies.

At night the sailors drink thick rum and sing out too loud every song the sea has ever heard. They do their singing at night because they cannot see what is out there. They cannot aim their sails very well, or swab the decks. They cannot use their eyes, which in this darkness try to be hands. Squinting in the dark, the sailors try to make their eyes feel ahead. Everyone does it.

The ocean at night is a whale-like cavern, but with the mouth of a tarantula, something unthinkable. One imagines the blackness and the movement to be many things. The night is beyond even the strength of the muscle a father makes for his son to see.

One will do anything to keep the teeth away, to keep the stars from coming down and the juice waters from coming up. Anything, any type of song, any kind of prayer. Because of this the sailor practices tying knots just to keep a rope near. Because of this a sailor practices knife-throwing just to keep a knife handy. Anything to use on himself, should the teeth of the night come together.

Sometimes the *Sirenas* answered the sailors back in song or in conversation. Sometimes their angry husbands all wet and foul-mouthed and careless drunk did the answering back to the sailors, and sometimes the sounds out there in the night were nothing at all.

THIS MAN WHO HAD come to town was a Triton. The townspeople were certain. Good or bad, one way or the other, no one could yet say. This was the story: he arrived in town from out of the dark, at night under a new moon, and no one had seen who or what had brought him.

He simply came to be at the front register of the two-room hotel, and laughed his laugh. No one knew how long he had waited before letting go of that singular noise, which sounded as if the stars themselves had come down from the night, so many little sparks, but without the light, so many little pinpricks in a row. No one knew how long he had waited, but the wait must have been long since so many sounds made themselves inside that laugh, so many sounds the laugh could not stop properly once it got started.

Armida, the hotel maid, led him away to one of the two rooms along the rollers of that laugh. Even when he closed the door, Armida said, she could still hear something of it. The laugh was full of small saws and bees, strong enough to cut through the walls and with enough wings to fly into the garden and along the street. Armida could not tell with any precision when it ended, or if it ever did. Some noises in that room in later years were simply unexplainable except for this.

When the man woke the next morning, Armida, the maid and the room service as well, said he ordered a *coctel de abulón* brought over to his room. I don't want it so much for the abalone, he said to her, as for the tomato juice and lemon. Armida nodded to him as if she understood, but she did not.

What he felt in his head was very big.

That is what the man said, she told everyone, as he had continued to talk. The townspeople who gathered nodded their own heads now. Something was inside the words he had spoken, but no one could yet say what. They nodded their heads, understanding only that if the man said something in his head was very big, then they had better get out of the way in case he let it out.

No one knew for certain how to interpret the man's words. Nor did they know their role as townspeople. Should they stay out of his way because they feared him, or stay out of his way because they had little interest in a visitor to town? That they should stay away was the only point needing no discussion.

THE TOWNSPEOPLE IMMEDIATELY CALLED the visitor Triton because, before he retired, he said something more to the clerk of the two rooms. He said either he was looking for his wife, or that he was looking for *a* wife.

The man moaned, and held his head. Then he laughed. Perhaps it was not a laugh at all, someone said. Perhaps they had mistaken the sound, and it was the moan he began with that had not stopped. A moan and not a laugh at all.

This made no one feel better, and no one wanted it as an explanation for anything.

This man had no drink at the bar, but that did not mean he had not been drinking. For that matter, he did not seem to have a gun, but that did not mean he was not hiding one. No one had seen horns on him either, but as they began to understand, that did not mean much.

Perhaps, they said at first, this man was only a bear, not something more. Things like this, a bear or a wolf passing through, things like this had happened before. Maybe he was just passing through, which would not be too bad. Or better, he was simply a vendor, with brushes or medicines under his greatcoat. A traveling vendor was something they had seen before as well.

The remark about his wife, however, or *a* wife, gave everyone second thoughts. Did this visitor know about their daughters? Should they hide them? The town had hidden people before. But no one knew what to do now.

Did he say anything about his wife singing, they asked both Armida and the clerk.

Had some one of their daughters sung too loudly, dreamed too much, or too hard? Had this Triton come to take one of them, who had called him without knowing? Had the tide of the ocean come up this far, so many hundreds of miles? In their Saturday evening talks they had often worried about the ocean. They worried about it coming up as far as the town some evening, not quite enough to swallow them all, but leaving one of its own lost to them. People knew for a fact stranger stories than this. And, as if by coincidence, many of them had to do with the ocean. So this story was possible.

Neither the clerk nor Armida could remember for certain whether the stranger mentioned any singing or any water. Perhaps he had said nothing, or perhaps he had.

AFTER HIS BREAKFAST OF abalone the visitor fell back asleep, snoring in much the same manner as he had laughed.

Mr. Lee was consulted.

The town had once saved Mr. Lee by hiding him from the soldiers who took all the Chinese and put them on trains. In return, he himself had saved the town, more than once. Though he said he knew nothing about strange occurrences, he always seemed willing to lend his ear to the moment.

Mr. Lee was brought over to the bar next to the two-room hotel where the Triton was asleep. Someone told Mr. Lee of the comparison between the visitor's laugh and a string of firecrackers.

He too nodded his head, but the townspeople felt sure that when Mr. Lee nodded his head *ahhh* it meant something different from when they themselves nodded.

Mr. Lee worked as a translator in this town. Every important document was taken to him for copying into Chinese, which had been a service to the community when there had been more Chinese in town. But since the trains took most of the Chinese away, the townspeople used his services differently.

The town hall had burned down two years previous, and Mr. Lee's job now was to translate various documents back from Chinese. He had kept his own library and at this point had the only town records left. When a question arose about some civic detail or other, Mr. Lee was consulted. He would go into his library and emerge with the appropriate document, which he would then bring back to life in a manner and language familiar to the townspeople.

On occasion, Mr. Lee's laws seemed different from what people could remember, but who could argue with the written word, regardless of its curvature.

From time to time, Mr. Lee himself would volunteer some arcane bit of law or other, some decision of the grandfathers for the good of the town. In this way, he showed them several new holidays, and with them he had the town order by special messenger a variety of foods that, somewhere in the business of everyday life, he said, people had forgotten—several roots for spice, some thin black sauces.

If anyone could discern something from the presence of this stranger, it was Mr. Lee. After all, the story of the Triton as mate to the mermaid had first come from a particular tapestry Mr. Lee owned, a tapestry with threads that shone.

The mermaids themselves came from the journals of Columbus. The further story of the *Tritones,* however, came with a little help from the dark inside of Mr. Lee's outer room. While he had not given Triton as the sea-creature's name in Chinese, that is what he called the thing for these townspeople. This was a name they would understand.

He had a mouth, this Triton, said Mr. Lee, which could blow hard enough to make a boat capsize. It was a simple example, but they each knew from experience what a boat capsizing meant. They supplied their own details. No one forgets this kind of story.

Suddenly this man appears, if he was a man, asleep next door, and with a laugh made from who knew what. It was cause for another beer, at the very least. A beer and a deep breath.

Mr. Lee nodded his head *ahhh* and listened to everything. By now each of the townspeople had something to say about the visitor. Each gave a new detail concerning the laugh, or said something about what seemed to take shape beneath that black greatcoat.

Who even wore a greatcoat around here anyway, they said to Mr. Lee in turn. Each had a different detail, but each had the same question. What was to be done?

BY NOW IT WAS time for the botana, the requisite social gathering of the townspeople in weekly celebration of Saturday afternoons. A little beer, a little food, some fried bits of one common thing and another, with tortillas, some *chicharrones,* then whole cucumbers with red chili powder and lemon and salt. A few prickly pear *tunas,* some purple ones and some green. A baseball game on the radio.

A hundred small pieces of conversation, an argument, which on these afternoons seemed like a large French bread, or better, a chair. Something there every time, but finally ignored. Someone in love, who wanted to be left alone. Some kids, who would eat quickly, not wipe their mouths, then run around drinking lemon-lime sodas, or shaking them and wetting the walls, seeing who could reach highest. Smoke, which was itself a second ceiling in this room. Some days it was a light cloud cover, some days a full cumulonimbus assemblage with a life of its own and animal shapes for the little kids.

Young people did not come to the *botana.* They were left to do chores at home. All of them, all alone, at home on Saturday afternoons. In truth, not much got done. Invariably the next Sunday a particular boy smiled at a certain girl a little differently. By some mysterious manner, some postal system not known to the grown-ups, they now knew each other better.

Who could say about these things. As everyone knew, however, and though they pretended coincidence, all the people who came for *botana* now had themselves met each other as youngsters on Saturday afternoons. They had met, and met often, when their own parents were off with their younger brothers and sisters to the great *botanas* of the earlier years in the century.

Mr. Lee had not a little to do with this, as he had clarified for the town that, indeed, these Saturday leisures were *de facto* the law. The law was a good one, the townspeople thought, after a while, whispering around their beers about things. It was their civic duty and good for business, talking things over and eating the small leftovers of the day. Progress worked this way. Who would not want to move forward like the new locomotives?

MR. LEE NODDED HIS head, ate a few of the shrimps and *tripas* from this *botana,* and listened to everyone. He summoned Armida and the clerk each in turn, and Armida would come back periodically with reports of what she heard at the stranger's door.

Mr. Lee sent a youngster to fetch his tapestry, which he then held up.

Did the visitor look like this? he asked.

The hour was dark, they said, and so late. Their eyes had been only half open, ready for sleep. As things turned out, only a few people had actually seen the man, and even then they had seen only his back. It was a large back, they agreed.

Armida and the clerk had seen him, however, from the front. They knew.

No, the two of them said, he did not precisely look like this picture in the tapestry. Not in the face, though he did have a beard. They could not look into his greatcoat, which he had kept well buttoned. This was at odds with the night, which was not so cold, said Armida. She was the maid and the room service, but her job was also to carry out the trash sometimes, or take one object or another outside at night. She spoke with the authority of many offices, and always with particular eloquence about the weather. Last night, I was out there, she said, and nodded her head from side to side—not so cold.

Not so cold, see, said the clerk. Armida says so. But this man, he kept that coat buttoned to the top.

Now, they said to Mr. Lee, look how long this Triton-man is sleeping, and in the daylight. Perhaps he is a creature of the night after all. Wasn't it possible?

Mr. Lee used his old explanation about these things, the one he used to explain everything that seemed curious at first. Without him saying so, it was an explanation from his own life. In putting on a belt in the morning, Mr. Lee said, a person should understand why another person somewhere else might be putting on a small dress of feathers, or how two artful sticks might be the equal of a fork.

At times like this, Mr. Lee always wanted to say a person is a person, but saying as much would have sounded too easy, too regular, not big enough. So he invariably took the long way around to explain this to everybody. We are all living out our days, he began. We do what is in need of doing.

Perhaps, if you will listen, our man's visit is not unlike *dim sum.* That is what others might call the *botana,* said Mr. Lee. Another people at another time of day, in another place, but these are the same thing. Different foods, different words, but the same thing. Perhaps, then, our visitor is just another man. Not like us, to be sure, but enough like us.

Mr. Lee shrugged his shoulders and nodded his head yes, once, firmly, which was also another way of telling them not to worry. Sometimes this kind of language worked better, letting people see an answer with their eyes.

Mr. Lee always came for the *botana,* he told them. He knew a good thing when he saw one. What they called it didn't matter to him— *botana, dim sum.* They could call it a purple people's picnic for all he cared. As long as they stacked up food on the tables.

Did they understand? he asked. This visitor had provided them with so many details, each so tasty, Mr. Lee said. Perhaps this was even a good man. Had he not been an entertainment, after all?

They nodded their heads in agreement. This was not the usual Saturday afternoon fare. This was true.

Firecrackers and pearls, stars and cowboy guns, unfolded serpents from the sea—Mr. Lee himself had paid good money to see these things at a theater in Nogales.

MR. LEE LOOKED AROUND and took a moment for his story. This was also the law, to tell one's story when there was one.

At the theater in Nogales, he said, as they all knew, Mr. Martínez played the piano. Mr. Martínez played the best he could, perhaps more with emotion than with a delicacy of hand. Mr. Lee said this with a wink, which they all understood. He played the piano to make the action seem stronger. You know—a fast piano for a fast horse. Sometimes Mr. Martínez fell off his chair, and was better to watch than the movie. At the very least, he was half the movie himself.

Just like an opera, Mr. Lee said. They had all heard Don Lázaro's records. A word said in an opera becomes a word spoken by someone who has swallowed a piano—a word with force, with music. Sometimes it was the movie talking, sometimes Mr. Martínez. Was he not in this way heroic, an equal to those on the screen?

Well, then, did they recall Señora Piñeda? She used to live here until her new husband moved the family to Guadalajara, then somewhere after that? The first several times she went to the movies, she yelled at the people on the screen to be careful! and not to trust the other one up there, not even for a moment. With Mr. Martínez up there, whom she had known all her life, and with all the action, shouting a warning seemed like the responsible thing to do.

Everyone nodded that they remembered her. More important, as seen in the quick tenor of their nods, they appreciated Mr. Lee's speaking only about her. It could have been any one of them. They had all yelped out at the screen also their first times. With the cowboys and the soldiers and the kings and queens up there, one could not help shouting, as a reflex, and as a friend.

AND THIS MAN MR. Martínez, said Mr. Lee, he did not even charge them anything at all for so many pleasurable hours. But to give away so much of himself was almost a crime. Of course, little did Mr. Martínez realize the entertainment was not in the piano. Still, no one could dare tell him, at least not anyone with upbringing.

They nodded their heads like Mr. Lee, *ahhh.*

Perhaps in homage to Mr. Martínez, to pay off their debt to him, the townspeople should offer this stranger something. Did Mr. Lee think so? Perhaps this was the way to make the world right. They could start off on the right foot again by paying this stranger for the entertainment he had provided, rather than letting the thing be unsaid, as was now irrevocably the case with Mr. Martínez.

Perhaps, said Mr. Lee. In homage to Mr. Martínez. As they were all friends of the Martínez family in those days, it was true they could not have insulted Mr. Martínez with the offering of money there on stage. They could not have made him bend down for something that was not a handshake, not in front of everyone else at the theater.

Leaving some gift now would be the thing to do, said Mr. Lee, a good way to remember. We should offer something to this stranger in appreciation of the lesson taught by Mr. Martínez. Did they not think so?

Heads were nodded, a bowl was passed, and a few beers went undrunk. After all, as Mr. Lee had said, paying for the services of an entertainment was the honest thing to do.

The clerk of the hotel thought the owner would go along with no charge for the room. After all, said Mr. Lee.

After all, they said.

Being scared had been good, Mr. Lee said, but not too good. Just right.

They nodded their heads in a slow *yes.* Nobody said aloud that the being scared had not quite gone away, or that they would leave early to check if their daughters were, at least, somewhere still in town. This Triton had done a good job of scaring them, and shaking it off would take a while. But they tried laughing, with Mr. Lee, and they felt better.

Armida was put in charge of leaving the bowl of money outside the door. The clerk would leave a note clearly stamped with the red PAID IN FULL on top of the bowl.

The plan was a good one, they all said.

This town, Mr. Lee said, while shaking his head. Here there was no need of wind, not with so many whispers, no sir. Were they not lucky living so close to nature?

At first they nodded their heads, but then they laughed. They returned to the strategies of the *botana,* declaring what should be eaten in turn, what was most medicinal, what was in need of salt. They remarked again on the striking aspect offered by the shiny threads on Mr. Lee's tapestry, which was still in the room, oversized with its full head of the Triton.

This brought on, again, the very first parts of the Saturday's conversation, Columbus, and his sighting of the mermaids. The *Sirenas,* they have done it to us again, everyone agreed. This was a music they had all heard, a fast melodic scale coming as if from the mouth of each of them, all about the stranger. These were melodies and harmonies perfectly meshed, coming as if they themselves were the half-fish and lived inside the sea, crying out to anyone who would listen for help. What a surprise their cries had been, and to have them come out like songs, so that everyone listened.

This is the way the conversation went, but it was not after all real conversation. The townspeople simply could not go away. Each waited to see if the man would leave, if the money and the hotel would be enough.

Underneath it all, the *botana,* the friendships, the stories, the beers and the *norteño* music, the afternoon air, and no matter what Mr. Lee said—underneath everything, and not to be rude, but *hijo de la chingada,* son of a bitch, they knew a Triton when they saw one. A laugh like that, so many pearls but without light, something from underneath the water, very far.

Real pearls leave a roughness in the mouth, not in the ear. Mr. Lee could make them feel better about the visit. But this man could not fool them.

A Trick on the World

LÁZARO SPAT INTO THE street, and crossed the avenue without looking. Who could accuse him of being the father of anything? Certainly nobody could believe him to be the father of the little girl María. An absurdity. He spit again to make his point, if only to himself as his own audience, as no one else was in sight. Who would have expected this?

He was not, however, a very good spitter and had to take out his handkerchief after the second time as not everything had left his mouth cleanly. He was glad not to have made his point too publicly after all.

Lázaro had been a young man not too long ago, and young men, as his mother had said many times, who can account for them? Today he tried to be young in that way again: he straightened his clothes and walked across the street with his chin held up at an angle, in that way he had seen others do, in that manner of the presidents. But he was not like those others.

He had never himself believed in their lack of accountability, in their license. And it was a license, like any other: they were allowed to do anything, as if it were their right. It was as if they had filed the papers properly, paid the two dollars, and received the appropriate and unassailable permit.

However, he thought. However.

Not so fast. Suddenly the license of young men—or at the very least, the license of brashness—in this town had a special bearing on his life, and could work in his favor.

There was a pregnancy, now, after all.

But who was he kidding, he thought, and a sadness took him over. He was not like those others, he thought again. His was not a sadness wrought by the possibility of being held accountable for the bringing forth of a child into the world. Quite the opposite.

Instead, his sadness was at being, if he could dare think it, so pleased at the prospect. If he *were* the father, then all right and three cheers. Forward with the cannons, he thought. Things like that. But he was not, in truth, the father of anything.

And yet, he was being held accountable as the one.

The situation was altogether confusing, and a little too big for itself. Some of it spilled out now and then through the day. Sometimes it was a small laugh for no apparent reason. Sometimes it was a spit into the street—all of it made of things he had never before done.

But what was not confusing was this: with regard to the making of a baby, he knew what was what. And he had not.

Not everyone was as well-educated as he, however, and for them there were many ways to make a baby, more than one of which he was guilty. Had he not walked through the years with each of the twenty young women his age, through the gardens of the park and into the low voices of the night?

In the eyes of many, a walk like that by itself was an impregnation, or even more. It was a marriage without papers, something understood, something from the centuries.

It was the binding of a book easy enough to read, they said.

Even the girls themselves, at least the first four or five, thought him to be guilty of making some promise to them by virtue of this kind of strolling together. It was almost too much for him to believe, until he had looked into each of their eyes a second time, and seen babies there.

In his view, however, they saw only roses and heard only whispers. This was a quietude, a joyousness for the moment. And that was all. It was a walk for the laughing they had taken, he would explain to each who asked him. It was a walk only, for love of the world, not for the making of more worlds.

A walk for the sake of walking. Couldn't such an easy thing be simply what it was?

There was a shrugging of the shoulders and a furrowing of the brow on their part, as if to say *no.* There was no such thing as an easy walk.

But Lázaro would shrug his shoulders as well, and therein lay his reputation as a terror in the town.

Imagine, people would say to each other.

Yes, would be the reply, *imagine.*

But I am a crazy man in a crazy time, thought Lázaro. It was true, so that no one after a while noticed him.

Until now.

Now he had to get people all riled up again, to make them see him once more as the boy who took the girls along the curtain of trees and into the evening. That boy. That kind of boy.

This was the plan, to pluck him up once more from the crowd, to get him known even better this time, to get people angry at him again. The plan was to focus everyone's attention on him so that the rest of the crowd could go on being invisible.

One of the crowd in particular. The plan was, after all, his—Mr. Lee's. And Mr. Lee was, after all, fortunately or unfortunately, Lázaro's best friend.

MR. LEE HAD NO first name. Which is to say, no one in this town could pronounce it. The name did not have any spelling with which they were familiar, so he seemed not to have one. Nor did he need one. Even when he was a teenager, arriving in this town for the first time, he had a particular bearing, an authority of ideas. *Mister* was used first with him even then.

That was what Lázaro called him now: *Mister.* And he called Lázaro *Lazo,* which was not a shortening of his name. This was simply how it came out of Mr. Lee's mouth even when he was fully saying the name. *Lazo,* or *Lazao.* It was something in between the two. Either way, it sounded like a cowboy's rope.

And a *lazo,* anyway, that was exactly what was used in weddings here, to show how two people are tied together when they marry. At the appropriate time, a silk rope was put around the bride and groom.

It made Lázaro shiver. A rope is a rope, after all. He had seen the movies. He knew what people in the movies used ropes for.

If the great, unknown outside of this town were once all green, out there in the distance beyond the hills, now it was an odd *grisaille,* as the French said. Or at least, it was what Mr. Lee said the French said, though he pronounced it *geesigh,* without the *r.* No green at all. Only shades of gray. As a way of living, not as a remark on the landscape particularly.

He had a gray feeling for himself, a little, thought Lázaro. It came from feeling sorry for himself, and for what he was about to have to do. But life was certainly all gray for Mister. And for the girl Jesusita. *Chuyita,* as Mister called her. And for their marriage, which would not be allowed here, not marriage with a Chinese.

Mr. Lee's plan for how to solve this problem of marriage between himself and Chuyita was a happy plan in the midst of unhappy times, or else the other way around. In fact, it was from the middle. It was more a sad plan in the midst of uneven days.

Lázaro could not say anything about it for certain. Every time he tried to figure any of his life out, his reasoning seemed to be more mixed up at the end than at the beginning. He feared that he was catching something of the fever of this town.

But if there was a possibility that these were happy days, thought Lázaro, then there should have been more laughter. More people wearing, who knew? Yellow pants. Something like that. Something good from the circus. Something ridiculous, but at least undeniable. These were yellow pants times, but with all their fever of what was right and what was wrong, the people of this town had the *grisaille.* They just didn't know it.

Oh, Paris, Lázaro would say, as if the comparison itself of Paris to this town was damnation. He imagined something else in Paris. It didn't have to be Paris, but the name worked as well as any other. It meant someplace else. Very far.

Oh, Paris. He could say it all he wanted. Nobody understood, and so they paid no attention.

Except Mr. Lee, who laughed every time.

Mr. Lee and Jesusita had already been secretly married. "We are in love, what else could we do?" asked Mr. Lee, nodding his head. That's all there was to it. He had a way of saying *love* that Lázaro liked, a sound somewhere in between love and laugh, *lough*. For such a thing as what Mr. Lee had pronounced, even Lázaro would have considered marriage.

The real marriage had been in Nogales, among the Chinese there. "Everything was taken care of, in the regular way for how Chinese were supposed to do it," said Mr. Lee. He and Jesusita had the official papers, everything signed. It had been night, after the regular hours, and the room had been properly dim when the magistrate entered, so that he could say that he did not see.

This kind of marriage cost a great deal of money, but there the deed was, in the record books of the government itself, and it could not be undone.

What would seem like a marriage of Jesusita to Lázaro, said Mr. Lee, would therefore be false, not legal at all. "A sam," he said, but meant his word to mean *sham*.

"A *sam,* good," said Lázaro, "I like that. A trick." Lázaro felt that way about marriage, but not just marriage. He felt that way about everything in this town.

He felt that his whole life had already been planned out, along with the master plan for this town, and for living in general. Even the way he dressed was measured by what was available and what he could buy to wear. A shirt was a shirt for everyone here, no exceptions.

And a marriage was a marriage.

"That is the plan," said Mr. Lee. "You must marry my Chuyita. Well, marry her more or less."

LÁZARO WALKED ONTO THE street into a soft rain. A gardener's rain, he thought, which is a whisper to the ground, a language unto itself. It is the soft rains that make the seedling grow, and it is the whispers that best make a baby. And it is the watching of two people in whispers that also makes the rest of the town grow to think a baby will be made as well.

That was the plan. That Lázaro and Chuyita should walk arm and arm through the town. From time to time Lázaro was to simply whisper into her ear. It would not take more than that.

Everybody would know what the whispering meant, especially coming from a man to a young woman. Whispering was by itself already the act of making love, so that anything which might happen later under the sheets was already redundant.

That's how the world worked here, simple-like but absolute. It was as if the truest sexual organs were the mouth and the ear, with a little help from the eyes.

That she would get pregnant, well, certainly. Who would doubt it? An experienced and handsome man like Lázaro. There would have been more talk had she not.

That he would not be so sure about marrying her, well, in this everyone stayed away.

Not in gossip, of course. But these were not the old days where a man might be shot for such an act, or more rudely be made to stand accountable in front of everyone. These were modern times, more or less, and who could say what should be done?

It was a sadness, of course. *It was just one of those things,* people would say to Jesusita's mother. *One of those things,* they would say with their shoulders in a shrug to her.

But the talking would have been worse had they known the truth. If Jesusita were made to say she had slept the night with a Chinese, well.

All right, then, they would have said. But everybody knew what would have to happen next. Though no one would say it outright, Mr. Lee would then be required to move to the Plano Oriente part of town, on the other side of the railroad house. It was the Left Side of Town, and needed no explanation.

He would have to live with all the others who did just these sorts of things. Mr. Lee would not be allowed to work in his business on this side of town any longer.

Who could trust him, after all? they would say. And being Chinese like he was.

Then to say Jesusita was married to Mr. Lee—that would be the end of things for the both of them. She would have to go and live with him, of course. Not even her parents could keep her any longer. There could be no trick of the night, no confusion of where one slept, not if they said out loud that they were married.

Their only recourse was to make a confusion of the night, but one nobody would find suspect, the best trick of all. This had to be something so big no one could see it. Theirs had to be something bold, yet invisible at the same time. Something from the circus. In this way they would find their lives together.

Everyone knew after all, that to be caught socially red-handed, a Mr. Lee of any kind married to anyone from a proper family here, would mean exile. And to be sent to the Plano Oriente, then work so hard just to visit this part of town, much less make a business, well. It was too much for this life. It was too much.

"After all," said Mr. Lee; he was already full of special permissions just for being Chinese anyway, and one more would make him too heavy, would make him fall over or look fat, which he was not.

"It would be too much to bear," and he would be able to make for himself no life, not to mention a life for Chuyita.

Lázaro understood that Mister was not talking about legal permissions or magistrate papers. He meant the social permissions, given and rescinded at a moment's whim. With whom one did business, well, in these first days of the town it meant everything.

Where is the honor otherwise? they would say. *How else can we be sure who to trust?* they would ask. There were rules. Or at least, there were manners.

LÁZARO AGREED TO THE plan. He began the whispering and the walks once more, along the row of trees where the sweethearts leaned. It was easy enough, since this was not the first time. And it was not something he had forgotten.

So everyone believed it.

In the afternoons while Mr. Lee caught up on his sleep, Lázaro and Jesusita would take their walks. Then in the evening, in one or another's house, Jesusita and Mister would spend their time together, and with laughter against the night. This was a town that slept at night. So, for those who did not, the world was theirs.

When Jesusita's stomach grew beyond honest response, the talking began, and the other kind of whispers. It was something Lázaro would say, and then say many times again throughout his life: small towns don't need any wind, not with so many mouths in service to a bit of imagined news.

I should not have bothered combing my hair, Lázaro would say. A walk in the park past the seated ladies, with all of their talk, would slick it right back.

"Still, who would really have believed they would all believe it?" asked Lázaro, finally out loud. "I confess I had reserved some doubts," he said to Mister. "The whole plan, well it seemed so impossible. That's why I liked it. But it was impossible."

"It's that you don't know what people were already saying," said Mister, and all three of them laughed at that.

Chuyita said, "I don't want to hear about such stories." She said she was just one more girl about to get her heart broken, and they all laughed again, but not as hard. This remark ended up leaning a little too much in the direction of what was truly possible after all.

"Thank you, no. No stories of sordid behavior," she said, to take the edge away from broken hearts. "Though I cannot imagine of what sordid behavior might be constituted," she continued. "Perhaps these young ladies gather after each of your adventures and discuss their various impressions concerning the size of your tie, or the waving around wildly of your, well of course, what else, your tongue...." The three of them, Lázaro, Mr. Lee, and Chuyita, could not stop laughing.

"But what has Lazarito gotten his tie caught in this time?" She said the familiar name of Lázaro, but with her hand she pulled on the loose necktie of Mr. Lee.

Everything was ready but for the moment itself. They had made the various necessary preparations, contrived the explanations, effected a provision for the baby's baptism in Nogales. It would work. They had chosen the name already, but only if the child were a girl. Of course the name would be María, said Chuyita. There could be no question. Mr. Lee and Lázaro both shrugged their shoulders.

"The government and Plutarco Elías Calles might have closed down the churches, but that's all," she said. "It will be María. That's all there is to it. That simple."

"Well," said Lázaro, "I don't know. It seems a little too much for me, a María being born of a Jesusita." But it was, after all, a twist. If only his other friend José could have been the father. That would certainly have been a mess of names, and something really for this town to think about.

The three of them, the names—it seemed crazy, all backward. And perfect, thought Lázaro. María and José and Jesusita. Only in a different order, Jesusita and José and María. Something like that, the Savior woman, the way some people thought it was anyway.

And why not, thought Lázaro. Practically a whole new religion in front of their eyes and no one could see it. A new religion, or an old religion. Who could say for certain.

"Well," said Lázaro, "perhaps a properly situated star will shine with extraordinary brilliance. It would save us a great deal of explaining about things like who is married to whom, I think. *On your knees,* we could say to everyone, and that would be that. Who could argue? A very brightly shining star could come in quite handy right now, don't you think, Mister? We could write a very good book about all this. We could call it *Sam.*"

Mr. Lee had certainly been thinking, but not about that. He had another plan.

"Opera records," he said. Only he said, "ahpa" records, and it sounded to Lázaro like "papa."

"Papa?" asked Lázaro with a question mark in his eyebrows.

"Yes," said Mister. "That's right. Opera records. The Boheme, the Carmelita. The butterfly. They will sound like they are covering the childbirth. You know. Have you heard them? The opera?"

Oh, Paris, said Lázaro, to himself. The sounds had been his refuge. He knew opera, all right. But he didn't know what Mister was talking about.

"Mister Mister. What in the world are you talking about?"

"You will be the papa. Or, you know, it will be like you are. Everybody will think so. You will play these records on the Victrola, very loud, and everyone will know. Or they will think they know."

"Know what?"

"That you are trying to cover up. You know. The sounds of Chuyita having the baby. The sounds of the baby. You know."

"Why would I want to do that?"

"Because then everybody will think you are trying to trick them. But they will be too smart. They have already seen for themselves Chuyita's stomach no matter how much we have tried to hide it. They think they know what is what, and they are not about to let us get away with anything." Mr. Lee was revealing the rest of the plan.

Thank God, thought Lázaro. There really did have to be more. No matter what they had said, it wasn't enough.

"And because they are so smart, they will figure out that you are playing the records so loud in order that nobody should hear the screams.

"They will think you don't want anybody to know that Chuyita is having a baby. So they will stay away.

"They will all talk, of course, because they will all know exactly what is happening. But they will stay away. They will let it happen.

"They don't want to have anything to do with this. Except, of course, to know everything. But they would prefer to hear it from somebody else. Or rather, to be the first to hear it from somebody else."

Mr. Lee had let it all out at once. There was something more than a plan here. There was something about how he felt, so he had to say it all quickly.

"And then what, Mister Mister?" asked Lázaro, half teasing but listening to everything.

"They will think you are going to take the baby away, because you do not want to marry Chuyita, you know. They will think somebody is going to take the baby, to adopt it for their own."

"Well, these things do happen. I *have* heard of it."

"Exactly," said Mr. Lee.

"But what will happen to the baby?"

"I will adopt it, of course," he said.

"If it looks Chinese, I will say it is my cousin's. Nobody will ask about that. The business of the Chinese is the business of the Chinese.

"And at the same time, if they ask what happened to Chuyita's weight, to her stomach, we will hint, you know how, with the sign of the cross and sadness on the face, that it died." With that, he looked at Chuyita, but turned his face away. It scared her.

"But they won't ask—you know. They'll just think they know, and say it to each other like truth, and nod their heads to each other, *stillborn.*"

The way Mr. Lee said the word, it sounded more like *stubborn* to Lázaro.

"But if the baby looks like Chuyita, well I will say that I have adopted it anyway, and point to the cash register. They will understand. They will think I took money from you, Lázaro, to take care of this child."

Lázaro took a deep breath. "But Mister, that's no good. They'll think you're terrible."

"No. They'll think I'm Chinese. You know, Lazo. You know how it is.

"It doesn't matter anyway. Then I will say I need help. A wet nurse. A baby-sitter. You know. They will understand why I will hire Chuyita as my assistant.

"They will look at each other and know." Mr. Lee could not stop his idea. "They will whisper," he said, "that, well of course, she was just recently pregnant, and wasn't it all just awful what happened, though perhaps this will bring her some consolation, but isn't the whole thing a tragedy from a novel, someone ought to be held accountable, and who does this young woman think she is kidding anyway, and their heads will be shaking back and forth the whole time."

Mr. Lee and Lázaro both looked at Chuyita, who was laughing.

"Wait a minute, wait a minute," said Lázaro. "They'll think you're terrible, but just think what they'll have to say about me."

"Just what they always have said," laughed Mr. Lee. "Or what you had wished they were saying. That this is your fiftieth or sixtieth child, that here you go again, and isn't it terrible, and what is it about you anyway that the young women are finding. You will be a hero of the big mouths. You will be famous forever. You will grow taller, and who knows what else. There will be a statue at the very least. It's a career, Lázaro, a job for you at last!"

Chuyita could not stop herself from laughing, and the two men could not help themselves either. Chuyita, however, was the only one of the three that moment to have a baby from the laughing.

LÁZARO PLAYED THE RECORDS all night, and when the baby came he almost did not hear it himself. The operas and the night became the same, loud and dark and deep. And even though no one in the town slept, the night still belonged to its regulars, who were not afraid.

Lázaro became fond of the records, and kept them for the rest of his life. Everybody knew his records. In later years, because he played them so much and so long, and since the baby that night was no secret, Lázaro would be accused of fathering all the children in this town. It was fine with him. He never married, not exactly, he would say. Why bother? But there was something in his eyes.

The records became so scratchy that in later years they began to sound as if the stories in the operas all took place in the rain. It was a general, easy, and regular rain, all the way through.

I know that rain, Lázaro would say. *It belongs there.* The sound in later years made him happy, though nobody could understand.

María del Carmen, they had called the baby, at first. And then María del Carmen Lee. In the end she looked like herself and found her own name.

Lázaro knew the sound of the rain, the gardener's rain, how it made its whisper to the ground, how it woke the seedling. He knew the whisper. And he would say it to himself, sometimes, as he listened.

Oh, Paris, he would say, quietly. And it was a promise after all. It held something. Something he did not have.

Oh, the grisaille. Then he would walk into his operas, and believe for a while he was there.

Champagne Regions

LÁZARO WAS SEARCHING FOR a peculiar March-yellow bird that had flown over the wall. He placed his hands on the top of the adobes, pulled himself up, and looked over.

But what Lázaro saw in place of the bird was the young woman Mariquita hanging out the white morning laundry, which was all wet but not beyond recognition. His breath was stilled in the instant, half from his weight and position of his stomach against the wall, half from what his eyes brought to him. Though she faced him, he did not think she had seen him. The wall here was in shadow, enveloped in the overhanging branch of a generous walnut tree.

Everything Lázaro saw at that moment over the wall gave him, how did he think it at the time: not heat, not precisely; not the brightness, exactly; something true to course, something positioned meticulously between the two. It was a champagne uprising of skin, this bubble lawn come to the surface, this momentary shivering of the shoulders after which his face turned red.

Shivering from hot or from cold or from what exactly, Lázaro could not tell. He remembered at that moment, half because of her and half because of the placement of his hands on the wall, getting gravel under his knees so many times when he was a boy. This moment was like that, just quick.

Who could explain?

The feeling came afterward, on his skin, on his arms and neck, the redness of his face.

What Lázaro did know instantly was that this feeling was from the time when heat Itself married flame Itself, how when it was done there was no turning back. Things from then on seemed to have always been that way. Before then, flame had been all spectacle, and heat a simple curiosity. But in good times and in bad now, fire was hot, not one without the other, no exceptions.

This was the moment now.

Lázaro could feel on his skin what he saw with his eyes: in profile, this young woman Mariquita bent forward. And from his angle behind the wall—and as she wore a loose-fitting cotton blouse—Lázaro saw her chest. He saw under her blouse the skin of her chest, angled into breasts. And he saw beyond that the champagne bubbling of her own skin there, at her breasts' ends, her dark nipples.

They were perfect in their lines, he thought, her nipples like Spanish flamenco dancer hats. And as hats, being hats, because they were hats, they gave the stark impression that her breasts would not ever, could not ever, be fully uncovered. In that sense, in this air of impossibility, he felt perhaps that he was not seeing what he was seeing.

But he was. Two, with movement, and at angles.

Lázaro saw, plain enough. Afterward he sometimes remembered not the moment, but what he imagined to be everything around it. The blue lavender, sometimes lilac, of the jacaranda trees, igniting in the tree limbs, burning the same slow burn of the inexhaustibly red bougainvillaea, as if all around him were the primal parts not of fire, but of what fire is made: that if they were to combine, or if he were to look at the branches and the leaves and this young woman Mariquita all at once, the mixture would be flame, something of the time just before heat and flame married.

But the moment was flame already, as Lázaro did look, could not stop looking. In the color also of the jacaranda was something he had seen once as a boy, something he should not have seen either, underneath the dress of a girl, the blue lavender of her personal laundry. Even as he thought of it there was still flame in the thinking, fire in remembrance. The flame of thought was married even then to heat forever, and here was the moment again, and he could feel it.

THINKING IN THE DAYS afterward about what he had seen was both exhaustion and dessert. Lázaro limited himself to one helping a day, and in that way preserved something of the rest of his daily life, some semblance of the workaday, of a body getting on, through breakfast, work and supper, through Church and the long Sundays where every effort to eat something cold was made by everyone, simply to cool themselves and keep the ruse of civility going. Perhaps pineapples. Ice cream, or rain sometimes. Something to be able to begin a Monday. Something to dampen the spirit just enough. Something to take the mind off a woman's dress or a man's moustache.

None of these tricks worked very well. Always the pineapples had fermented, the ice cream made people happy, and the wine led to champagne. The rain simply drew people together under umbrellas or the overhangs of dark buildings.

LÁZARO DECIDED HE MUST apologize. The young woman he knew as Mariquita could not know that he had seen, and yet he could not deceive her. An indiscretion must be accounted for. In this purgatory of his, everything was as promised: close to heaven, but very hot. Lázaro did not suppose this to be the lesson he had learned as a child at his catechism, not exactly.

But here he was nonetheless, a soul tortured by the sugar joyfulness of something that should not have been done. He could not say it, but he could not forget it. In Mariquita's general presence at the park on Sunday afternoons, when Lázaro knew she was there—as how could one not know such a thing—he drank his coffee black, and still, because of seeing her again, the coffee was too light in its color and sweet to the tongue.

A good coffee, after all, is the one taken in the company of a friend. It owed little finally to the particular bin in the *mercado* from which one drew with precise measure a kilo of Cariculillo, or a Tapachula, depending on the morning and how one felt. They may as well have been called, for him, by their real names, these coffees: Mariette, Julia, the girl who showed him the reeds along the turn in the river bank, and the late summer sounds the reeds could make, properly placed in the mouth. It was not the coffee by itself, but with whom these particular coffees had been drunk.

Here at this wall he had found something of her again. Not the same girl, to be sure, not Mariette or Julia, but something from the moment: looking over the wall's edge and in seeing this young woman, there was a sound in the air, and the smell of coffee. But it was all inside him, as if, he thought, smoke would come from his ears and the national anthem from his nose. Right here was that coffee of his Sundays, which was desire.

This she, after all, was the young woman whose name he dared not say aloud for fear of being incapable of further speech. She walked by him on Sundays along the benches in the park, but he could say nothing.

Because of who she was—mixed together with his shortness of breath—Lázaro felt capable only of swallowing her name before anyone could take it from him, the time it would linger in his mouth, for the moment being his. And in doing so he would be swallowing her, the here of her and the seeing of her, and the lines of laundry as well. Even her laundry he could not forget. And with all that in his throat, no wonder he could not speak.

It seemed as if, he thought, at any moment she would turn and find him out. And once again, how would he explain his eyes? This moment was all accident, but what could he explain?

One way or another, somewhere in this heat a fine pastry was being made, a dough rising as he had not known, though he was the town baker. These goose pimples, he thought, were just the beginning. The time was right. If he were to do nothing, he knew, he would burn. Here was the marriage from the centuries, heat with flame.

But it was all him, and this was, if Lázaro might say so, a problem. She, after all, did not know.

And yet, when Lázaro got close to Mariquita on Sundays, casually walking by her, or sitting in her vicinity, this is what happened, a sound in the air and the smell of coffee. He thought, how could she not know? This is no trifle, this capacity of hers to put him close to danger, either from explosion or foolishness. Normally, he thought, this would be grounds to call in the police.

But *no,* it went without saying, *no.*

LÁZARO SET ABOUT ON the very next Tuesday to confess all. I have seen underneath your shirt, everything there is to see, he would say to her. Maybe. He would beg her pardon, an act of fate he would say, a dark yellow bird never before seen this far south, then offer her the brim of his hat and walk on, strong in his path, away.

The brim of his hat. His hat, he thought. In touching it he might be suggesting something beyond custom. Lázaro sat on his bed, and looked at his hat, the bowl of it. Resting his eyes on its lines, for a moment and in that light— that peculiar light at this time of the morning—and with his eyes squinting, he saw that the hat looked like her. In its bearing and in its careful molding, it looked like her. Like her There, under her blouse. His hat.

Lázaro shook his head, at first to get rid of this trick of the dawn. But then he shook his head again, to try and bring the image back. His own hat, he thought. The hat belonged to her. Could he wear it again, and at its angles and postures—could he touch with his hands what belonged absolutely to her? He didn't know.

This is too much, Lázaro thought, and resolved thereupon to make his walk in the park without the hat. How could he not have noticed this through the years, this—what could he call it, he wondered—this billboard, this advertisement of himself, this sandwich board on his head. Could it be he had worn his desire so obviously? Could it be that all the men were so blatant, and that he was simply another regular one of their ranks? Could he be so much like his brothers and like the other men in this town without knowing?

Did they all know what was going on—was this another trick of these very brothers of his, who would do just such a thing and then laugh behind his back? They must all know, Lázaro thought, with certainty. Was this, then, the secret signal between a man and a woman, chancing to meet, this light touching of the hat, and her smiling? Had he been so innocent through the years of so carefully minding his manners?

Or perhaps his tipping of the hat had, by sheer luck, made Lázaro seem wiser and more modern than the others, as he did it without fail, and boldly. Perhaps there was reason not to laugh at him. Perhaps that is what he had made them all believe. Could they believe him expert in the ways of the world? Well, possibly, he thought. Quite possibly. No one had, after all, laughed at him.

Lázaro resolved therefore to revise his original plan, deciding this time to in fact wear his hat on his walks. That it was a fine hat, as it suddenly occurred to him, made him shiver.

LÁZARO ROSE FROM THE bed intending to begin his toilet, but Pope Urban VIII knocked at the door, that way he had learned with his tail. Yet what Lázaro saw when he looked down at the dog was not the Pope's tail—it was his nose, dark, at the end of his snout.

This cannot be, Lázaro thought, as though the dog's face were not a face at all, not any longer, perhaps never having been. Seeing this dog's nose felt like getting a telephone call, thought Lázaro: suddenly, there was a voice from nowhere speaking.

This was not Mariquita's voice, admittedly, calling to him, as if she were using the laundry lines instead of telephone wire. But looking at the nose of the dog felt like a telephone ringing: Lázaro, on the countenance of the dog, saw in the darkness of its snout something remarkably like what he had seen under her blouse. This was her, in the way a telephone voice is immediately recognizable.

Was there some network, he thought again, some language of words no one had spoken to him before, some kind of netherland telephone he had never used, or perhaps never recognized? Was there some working Parisian Metropolitan of fare-paying desires traveling between the legs of everyone in this town, the way one might ride a horse? An underground railway between smiles on two passing faces, or a telegraph in footsteps perhaps?

The Pope barked, and Lázaro let him out, but gave him a sidelong glance, to be sure. Perhaps the dog had been hired. Had Lázaro given himself away—had the dog been alert, had it noticed too much surprise in his face, his eyebrows jumping, for a second or two, several inches into the air upon seeing a breast where a cold nose should have been?

Not to be made the fool, he gave the dog a push forward and closed the door with authority.

Upon turning around, Lázaro surveyed the room. He did not want to make too sudden a movement, readying himself to be certain another revelation did not take him by surprise. He moved his eyes like a comb, but suavely, like a gangster, as if without concern or motive. But he felt panic. Lázaro was on to them, whoever they were—but were they on to him as well?

Being in this room, familiar and unfamiliar in the

same second, felt as if, thought Lázaro, he were once again at the theater in Nogales—in *The Wizard of Oz,* how from nowhere suddenly there sprang faces and bodies, hundreds of little people, all of them laughing those high, needle-like laughs.

But this was no movie, or if it was, there were not yet any muffled sounds of laughter. Not yet. Lázaro closed his eyes for a moment, but his other eyes took over, the ones on the inside, as if they had been waiting, an ambush almost, a moment he could not believe, blackguards, running him, as only the eyes closest to dream are capable, past the tops of the town's street lights, over ice cream cones, over the five spinning tops from his boyhood. Over a lit candle.

There were women everywhere in this place. And candle flames suddenly.

Fire he knew about. Lázaro had fully expected to burst into flame himself on any number of occasions not entirely dissimilar from this moment—as in his secret times, alone but not alone, in the way a mind is capable of imagining. So to find himself taken suddenly over a candle flame and to be asked to believe that a breast could have as its center a flame—this was not too much to ask.

Not that he was complaining. His abduction into dream and by his second eyes was, after all, though he could not say so, a good tour, something European. As if from a brochure, this was a tour he would have considered: this place so big and with light, the moon itself on the single breast of night, two eyes, eyes themselves, eyes, sometimes with blue nipples as well as brown, who would have thought?

All this was a surprise, and all at once, so many things his own eyes had brought home through the years now being called forth and held accountable, held to inspection as if against a light bulb. It was like in the movies, any war movie, when the Commandant suspects there is information held among the prisoners, the way he has them rousted out and made to stand for hour upon hour until someone finally breaks.

There is a sadness then at someone having broken, but a relief, too—one must look hard for this—among his fellows, who understand, and yet cannot catch themselves thinking that they understand, cannot in the midst of war find relief but in secret.

The truth is, they all know the answer. The erasers on ends of pencils. The particular knobs on his chest of drawers. In all of this, Lázaro was on to something.

WHEN POPE URBAN KNOCKED again, the very two knocks themselves, the two sounds they made, added to the new equation. Lázaro opened his eyes and found that he had fallen, not into sleep, but into instruction. The world, he could see, was new in its oldness.

Waiting for the dog by the door and closing his eyes, Lázaro had held his face against the doorjamb, and he rubbed his cheek to take away the lines. In doing so Lázaro felt the necessity to shave, and so began his day again. He moved toward it, with comb, with toothbrush, a small breakfast of breads.

Of course he knew that an apology is most often delivered at the front door, but that would not do. Lázaro felt certain Mariquita would not understand what he was talking about if he went simply to the front door.

And so his walk delivered him, without fanfare, along the same route, behind the fence, the way the original bird had led him. Quietly. It was the only way, to show her how it might have happened the first time, to recreate the scene so as to show its plausibility.

True to his plan, reaching the wall, Lázaro could hear Mariquita at work inside the yard, could imagine the whiteness again of this business of the Tuesday morning laundry, the private nature of white cottons. He could imagine the lines and the wooden clothespins, the appearance of everyday clothing put up, and in that way the world seemingly turned upside down and inside out. Lázaro considered for a moment that he understood this worldly condition of laundry.

But it came to Lázaro also that he might look over the fence once more, in an honest effort to make his apology and to show how his seeing her could have happened. But it also came to him that when he did look, Lázaro would—with his peculiar brand of luck—show his head at the moment when Mariquita again would be bent. In his direction, blouse open enough, and everything there. By everything, Lázaro meant everything, the whole world, as he had come to see.

How would Lázaro explain this as a second visit then, as an apology? How would she construe his courtship?

Lázaro's looking over the wall a second time would not then seem sorry in its intent at all. An apology might seem like pretense, as if he had come for more and simply gotten caught, apparently knowing the work plan of the day behind those walls.

Lázaro's looking over the wall a second time might seem as if the one time were not enough, or that there had been many times—when in fact last Tuesday had filled his life with room for nothing more. Who could explain the entire and necessary world's fitting into what he had seen and felt? Who would understand?

Lázaro could not move his back from its place against the wall.

He was neither happy nor unhappy, but willing to let the moment simply be, willing to let the beaks of the fat birds, hunched above him and squat against the morning cold, be what they were, be what everything was, breasts at song. Birds after all were some of those many things that escape from dream, that get away and break out, and in that way can be again, in an instant, what they were in dream, not pigeons at all, but witnesses to the course of desire. And what after all was not desire?

For Lázaro today the birds were his old friends. He recognized them. They had with their songs and their real beaks pinched and torn at the edge of his sleep, enabling their escape. But in so doing, they caused the diaphanous walls of the thin room of dream to deflate like a balloon, the fury of this small explosion allowing the sides of this thin structure to envelop him, to fall over and onto him, so that everything for him at this moment was dream.

Odd dream, new dream, impossibility. The way a solid red brick cannot be so perfect, but is. The way Mariquita hummed a small song, because at her breast, he thought, a small song was everything.

Mr. Todasbodas

In the late Twenties and early Thirties, José Martínez was a carpenter of note. He was also, as they said, a man who liked to get outside the house. Everyone knew the color of his tongue, and the condition of his teeth, as he loved to chat idly with people. This second job of his did not always mix well with the exacting demands of carpentry, his choice between the two being the carving out and sanding of a fine, home-made story, elevated to the art of scrimshaw.

The story behind his stories was that his wife Rosa had to hide things. They were poor, without much of anything but his mouth and her determination. For example, the few photos of their girls, photographs in those days being expensive and uncommon, Rosa would have to hide from José.

His habit of talking was such that he was likely to take a photo out of the house in his shoe or underneath his belt. Thereupon, he liked standing on corners, and everyone would pass. Don José loved then to talk about the photos, their circumstance and their nuances, but upon finishing he would not always bring them back. He would lose them, or forget. Often, just the getting them out of the house would already have damaged them. He would do all this just to have something more to talk about.

He would rather talk than work, but Rosa would make him work. In that way he was responsible. It was that simple. He could be counted on, sooner or later, to do what Rosa told him.

He was very good at making furniture, and cabinets in particular. His preference for cabinets came from their placement in kitchens, where a conversation was always the best meal in the house.

But because of the Depression, and the Revolution to the south, and other big words and big ideas, there was little real work in these years. When times were slow, a regular secondary source of income for him was to work for the funeral home in town, because in those days funeral homes would hire out for everything, including carpenters, whom they kept on call.

They would require the carpenter to make the coffin right away because people had to be buried as quickly as possible—they were not filled with preservatives then, as science was somewhere between the Egyptian call for sand and the modern liquids. Often people took their dead home for a quick last visit and look around, and this also took up some time, but who could say no?

This being the case, the funeral home job was not a nine to seven job, and often he would work through the night. The carpentry shop was attached as if it were a cousin to the funeral home, and one day José got a call that one of the old Mr. Lunas had died, whom he did not know but who lived on Huatabampo Street with Lázaro, the old man's nephew.

José and Lázaro had been friends since childhood, but they saw little of each other these days. Still, José was sorry. It occurred to José that not meeting the uncle was surprising after all this time, but there were just so many damn Lunas, he thought, it was hard to keep track. Perhaps they had met after all, José reasoned for a moment. But no, one did not forget a face from this family.

José was called, he started to work, and this is the story he later told.

HE STARTED ON THE coffin. He finished sawing, had begun sanding, and was almost finished. He was by himself. A smell of sawdust and carnations, of oak and of rose, filled the room. It was late at night. José was a practical man, and not nervous about doing what certain other carpenters would not.

In the same room that the coffin was built, the funeral home kept the body that would be going into the box, at a distance, on a table, covered as a body should be. On this night, Mr. Luna the dead man was not close, but was within Don José's view.

In the beginning, José shouted over as a courtesy, How are you, Mr. Luna? I am happy to meet you after so much time. I know your nephew. Perhaps he has mentioned me to you.

And that was all. It was a way of asking permission to begin with his tools, and was something he felt.

José had been working for a while, and did not remember any longer that the body was there, probably because it did not talk back to him and so served him little use in what he counted important in life. The reason bodies were kept there was a practical one, as that was also where the family dressed and combed the body, and the less the distance between fixing and transportation into the coffin the better. A groomed body is a groomed soul, and therefore more welcome in heaven.

Or if someone had taken a body home, it was a good place to say good-bye, a room like this, with sawdust. A real place, without all the hard music that pretended to be soft, and flowers and tears, which come from somewhere else.

Suddenly José heard a noise, a creak, and since the room was otherwise so silent, he knew he could not be mistaken. He stopped what he was doing and he looked across the room. As if it had just heard Don José, as if it had been hard of hearing, as if in conscience and because of manners it could not let the earlier address go unanswered: The body sat straight up—Mr. Luna, introducing himself finally, famously, making with his head a motion to the side, with a spitting sound, and he spit up what was or used to be blood.

Mr. Luna's head turned back, and he eased down again. Nothing else.

José dropped everything, streaked from the room, and went straight back to Rosa, saying in very obscene language, explaining in no uncertain terms, he was never going back there to work. Had he thought the moment out, he might have said more boldly that he was simply never going back to work, but the moment escaped him.

Rosa said, but José, what happened, what happened?

Don José, with obscene words, not directed at her, but not controllable either, said no ma'am, no way he will go back.

He told her finally what he had seen, and he himself looked as all white, as all frightening as the Mr. Luna he described. He could not have known it, but he would have been describing himself had he looked in a mirror that moment.

Rosa kept trying to talk sense, there must be a reason, she said, and other things like that.

He did not care, this is what he saw, something that should not be seen, did she understand that, something he wanted no part of.

But they needed the money, and this was an oak coffin, she said, trying to say so with force.

DON JOSÉ WAS CALLED down to the neighbor's, where he received a call from the funeral director, his boss, why was the work not finished, come back immediately, finish the work you have begun, Don José, you are the best at this, need I tell you again ...

José explained to him what he had seen, what he should not have seen.

The owner said, Don José, that's nothing my friend, I've seen that happen, it happens now and then, you know, it has a scientific name, do you want me to find it? They were just gasses, well you know, like from beer, it's because he is dead, and they build up like that in a corpse. I've heard they can explode, but I've never seen it. Not myself. But no. Nothing to be afraid of.

The man could not soothe Don José.

It causes motion, all those gasses in the body, that's all. A motion, so like you say, sometimes they sit up, like that. It doesn't mean anything. Now I need you to come and finish this job, you started it, you'll be wanting the money, don't you think? Have you told Rosa? It's an oak coffin, after all, did you forget? Should I speak to her perhaps?

José, in need as he was, in need as his family was, just told the man never.

Dead people don't get up, he said. He refused to go back.

It made Rosa unhappy to hear him, as this coffin making was one of their few sources of real income in those hard days, and too bad he wouldn't reconsider, wouldn't he reconsider? José, the money. Look at our girls. José. And it was oak, had he forgotten?

He had worked there a long time. He was their carpenter, the favorite of the funeral director, an expert, José had said more than once in any number of stories.

And wasn't he afraid, they would say, and no, he would shrug his shoulders, certainly not, of what would he be afraid, after all? And they would shake their heads.

Rosa was the hard one in their marriage. He was the playful one. Their daughters liked him best, and Rosa took in laundry, grew a pig and some chickens, and butchered them because she couldn't count on her husband, not the way her daughters could, not for the same things. She could count on that she could not count on him.

Rosa would gather and save extra money, only a little, but it was extra, because if she didn't, well she knew by now, after so many years. There was always a need. There would always be a need.

She could never tell José about it because he would take the little bit of money to go and buy everyone drinks, tea or coffee, a *limonada,* a *cebada,* or liquor if they preferred—he was not himself a drunkard particularly, his irresponsibility did not come from the smile of the worm in the bottle. His drink was the red *jamaica.* But he was simply casual with money, whether he had it or not. He had family money growing up in life, it was rumored, but no one could say for certain, only that such being the case would explain a great deal.

Rosa always liked to garden, but José was lazy, and didn't care for plants very much. She would go to this extent, because her husband would not: when she got money from her chores, from taking in ironing and laundry, the garden was the one place she knew he would never go. If she found he had worked because someone would tell her, even though he would deny it, when he fell asleep—he was a sound sleeper—she would search his shoes for the money. Then behind his belt. His favorite places.

She wouldn't take it all, but just enough. When he awoke, neither one said anything. He was guilty and so was she, but there was nothing to be said. He had not worked, and so she had not taken any money. ·

Then she would bury it in boxes in the garden. Her own coffins, next to the zinnias, or the snapdragons, which is what he sometimes called her.

AT THE END, HE left Rosa to live with another woman. He left for ten or fifteen years, going farther south into Mexico. He disappeared. He was never heard from. Just like that.

Until one day suddenly he reappeared, the same way he had gone. He was considerably older than Rosa. By now, he was in his late seventies, and she was in her early sixties. He would call all his grandchildren his *conejitos,* his little rabbits, which they would always remember. He was very fair and had a blonde moustache, so that everyone called him *güero.* He was not tall. Slender. One of the daughter's daughters would marry a man who, she always said, looked like him. They would remember Don José as tiny and bent over. They would remember that he made them laugh, and talk very little about the rest.

A *todasbodas,* they would call him, a Mister All-weddings, an all-parties, even when there were none. There was a something, they would say, a tuxedo, in Don José's eyes, so that he was always ready to go. Even at the end.

He was very ill, and knew he was dying. He did not come home to be a burden, he just knew he was dying and he wanted to die by her side, he said to Rosa. He had no other explanation.

She said, he was her husband, and she took care of him until he did die, two years later. It was the 1950s, and everything was different, and everything was the same.

BUT THIS WAS NOT a story about Rosa. Though she would have liked to take it over. To buy it off with her extra money, saved for something just like this. The Old Grapefruit, José would say to himself. The Old Lemon. She would love to have this be her version of the story.

Life is funny that way, letting a beautiful green tree with white flowers grow grapefruit. Well, who could explain. That Rosa, he would say, as he perched himself precariously backward in his chair, holding his glass of red *jamaica.*

She wants me to go back, he told them all the next day, can it be imagined? What you all said was true. There is reason for worry, after all. You were right, he said, and they began to gather around him.

But Don José, they said, we didn't believe anything could happen. Not truly. We were just talking, you know how that is.

No, said José, no, you were right, altogether right. I should have listened, but I'm bad about that. I have small ears, I think. I don't hear very well. They used to be big, but

Rosa, you know, so many years, so many words, so much yelling. They used to be big cabbages, and now, what, I think they look like little snails. They crawl around on my head, you've seen that. When Rosa has been shouting at me, I let them crawl over my nose to fool her, so that she is yelling into my nostril. That's when I put my ear to the coffee, and listen to its steam. It has a great deal to say.

Your coffee talks, Don José?

Certainly, he would say. Are you a child, have you not listened to your coffee, he would continue, and they would laugh.

But today he told no jokes, not at first. There was a scare in him, and they could see it, as if his eyes—in the manner of his ears—had tried to step back, finding themselves trapped against the wall at the back of his head, no way out.

And his moustache too for a moment and before they remembered the redness of the *jamaica,* that a tea like that might stain the light hairs of a moustache, his fine moustache seemed to drip a slight rim of blood, as if his lips too were trying to tell this story.

No one could say for certain whether this had happened, this story, this miraculous rising of the famous Mr. Luna.

They believed it could happen, and had warned Don José many times. It was their worst nightmare about the funeral home, and what went on in there. People passed by it only on the other side of the street for fear of exactly what Don José had related.

But to have Don José actually say that it actually happened, well. There was shrugging of the shoulders and a general lifting of beer glasses and sipping through straws, some coughing, some rolling and curling over of the lower lip.

Don José saying that it happened, well, that was the thing.

They found themselves not believing what they believed, feeling themselves put on by Don José, feeling that he had been right all along, such a thing was unthinkable, impossible, the legacy of the gypsies from the south. They found themselves laughing, and all the more as they saw how serious Don José was looking, how put upon and abandoned.

He was the best, they said, and they bought him his next drinks, with pleasure.

José himself no longer knew what was true and what was not. He had, after all, sat in this chair so many times, leaning it backward in a boy's dare of gravity, and told stories halfway true and halfway from inside his left leg, as if having put photographs in his shoe had been like the planting of seeds, and as he walked something sprouted up, into that very leg.

The hard thing for him was that Rosa herself believed him this time, and was the only one. She believed both that it had happened, and that he was frightened. She could recognize the *susto* that people sometimes get, and then cannot shake off.

José knew that she believed him because he could see she believed that somebody getting up after dying was fully possible. He saw that she believed it out of her own meanness and determination, that if she thought something was still to be done at the end of her life, dying would simply be an inconvenience in accomplishing the task.

After he left for so many years, he knew he had to come back, because he knew her to be capable of rising from the dead. He knew it from the sourness of her grapefruit face, how this was a badge of her determination. He understood her to be capable of sitting up herself when she passed away, of sitting up and standing, and walking, walking and asking questions and then directions, until she found him, and dragged him back home by his ears no matter how small he made them.

His voluntary return was simply to forestall the inevitable. It was his way of saving the world, he thought. And regarding his own life, well, son of a bitch.

Sawyers Along the River

THROUGH THE WINDOW A breeze left over from the cool night woke him, combed him, lifted him a little, then pushed him toward the door, which seemed to him larger than the night before, and heavier.

Mariquita waited for him. A name so plain, María, Mariquita, who would think anything of it, he thought. Who would think she could move the way she did in his mind, like a fish caught and held out of water, that much commotion, that much disturbance, an excitement gleaned from somewhere on the edge of life itself.

He had disappointed her not a single Tuesday for the last six years, nor she him. At their meetings, though he imagined them as fish out of water, they were not. He imagined them wild, but they could not be. Someone might see them. So their meetings to the world would have looked like a smoothness of life, something casual, something happening that might just as easily not have happened. This was their trick on the world.

HE READIED HIMSELF WITH the attentions of a younger man, a little too long at the task, at a mirror a little too big for his needs. Always on Tuesdays an hour was an hour no longer, in the same way that the simple steps he took to get to her house were not the same steps he took to get to the government buildings or to Molina the butcher's. They measured the same on a ruler, but only there.

Still, this morning he seized the day not with his hands but with his forearms, more awkwardly but more fully, with more strain to his muscles. This was that moment in the morning sometimes ascribed to increasing age, but which has nothing at all to do with getting older. Something in his blood was making the walk slower toward his heart today, something making everything in him feel slower. But this was not age. It was something else, something considerably more forceful.

Who could not think so, and yet who could he tell? Theirs was a—could he call it something more than friendship? But this was a friendship like no other, in that no one in this town knew of it. This was something all their own, a privacy, a lingering without explanation. The families did not know. The town did not know, as there had been nothing in the newspaper, which here was a newspaper of nuance rather than bold headline.

The world mattered, so to speak, but what the old Don Lauro had said to his daughter-in-law two years previous, for example, meant more. This was the sort of news the paper carried, though it might not be evident on the front page. One read the paper here back to front, going from what mattered to what was simply news.

THEIR MOMENTS INSTEAD WERE from somewhere in a fifth season of the year, and so the fact of their meetings was not fact at all. As no one knew, and the papers had not breathed it, their meetings did not exist. So he had told Mariquita, and with that little allotment of the supernatural she was satisfied. This was a good life, to be in love with nothing.

Their act of love through the years was simple: he would say his several quick words, and in return she would kiss him. How can anyone not believe in God with evidence of his heaven so plain, he would say to her, after which she would give him the kiss, or else he would say it was the *sing* in *kissing* that stood him most in awe.

These were the words, unrepeatable in the company of anything more than two, and even at that a risk. Small truths and small lies, woven into a fabric at least as strong as cotton, something durable, wearable, able to stand the strain of years and able to hold in the evidence of desire.

But it was the inside of a garment that was their love. An inside, where no one could see; where the stitch lines were most visible, and the flaps of cloth hung; the inside of a cotton pant leg—this was the moment. Where the real workings were, the more startlingly clever and inclever secrets of sewing, the fineness, the firmness, and the mistakes. Hidden here, still serviceable, still a fine pair of pants to the world on the outside.

This love was the same way one got lost in the very large backyard gardens, a hundred years old, so many green cut-outs and backdrops, so many flavors of the smell, so much rose. And the walk on insolid ground, on the forgiving eucalyptus-leaf-and-rosemary-tine mulch that redefined street, this avenue of the small woods.

Here was the entry place to memory, and the making place of things toward future. All loam, it seemed not by itself anything, but everything was there: the place one remembered going and hoped again to go, the single mulberry giant in a field full of cows, house-like in proportion, with limbs as wide as roads, full in season with its purple and red thousands upon thousands of earring-like fruits, a tree for the dancing, for the late summer music, dressed in its red dress and ready.

It was never the present, for one sensed an immediate transportation. And this was what her kiss was, then, the fabled machine of time: this was the kiss, the small, light, noiseless finger-snap of lips. Her kiss, for him.

This exact Tuesday kiss, which did not exist for the world, and which in this town could not be told, was the loudest thing imaginable, but in a town of the deaf.

In him was always the fear that someone would hear its tenderness, which is to say, that someone would find them out. The feeling was so much that it must be loud. And what he could not bear was the thought that this remarkable clock, this kiss of Tuesdays, might end. Or worse: that it might be changed, that the hands of this clock might move in some other manner, something slower, or something more encompassing, some movement that might include the other days of the week, some movement toward the unbending business of the regular.

To avert that possibility, he took many and varied measures, each as different as the words he would later say to her. Not false moustaches, to be sure, nothing like that, so obvious even to the dogs. No overcoats in summer, nor winding walks with furtive backward glances to see who had followed. He did not use the back doors of morning cafés.

He did only what was plain. His walk was his walk, with nothing at all to distinguish it but that he never failed his mornings. He did not sing, and yet neither did he fail to sing; his was an even keel as the fishermen said, in between one thing and the other, a true plane as the carpenters said, unnoticeable, serviceable, neither quiet nor loud, just there: invisible in its unremarkable simplicity of balance. Nothing, of course, was further from truth, since when was balance not a remarkable thing—did one not spend money to be made to pay attention to it at the circus? And therein the genius of this man spoke, not in words. The even walk of an even man.

On Tuesdays, artlessly, routinely, he would turn right instead of left; he would walk a half block farther north, thereby walking behind the back wall of her family's house, to the side of the trash bins, until he stood by the misaligned garden gate, where the tools and sundry small machines for gardening were kept, under the shadow of a morning-sun shelter. There she would wait for him, on the pretext of necessary pruning shears.

Under the shade of the twin jacaranda trees, lilac with blossoms in summer, between the large-leaf hedges, behind the grape vines and before the towering oleanders, to the side of the bloodflowering bougainvillaea and ferns in the humid hum of the shade: there he would find her, remove his walking hat, say his words; there, she in her turn would find him, listen to his words, or rather, watch his words, then kiss him the kiss of that second which is an hour.

They found themselves there in that same spot every time, or sometimes it was to the left a little, but just a little. After the kiss quickly she would turn her attention with shears thereupon to the garden, as he would replace his hat and continue this walk of years, to the bakery.

And yet he might well have been riding in a car. Inside him the engine and the pulleys, the pinwheel and the smoke, they were all strong at work. The wheels on his feet, the air parted by the shear of his absolute movement. The ride of a car all new.

TODAY WAS DIFFERENT. SOMETHING else was at work. Some other kind of motor, something nearly in reverse, and stuck there, and whining in its grind.

He was reminded of the great thunderstorms of summer, after which the trucks with great comic capacity would get stuck, turning their wheels in any of the assorted number of holes filled with sludge on any number of streets, mud which invariably found its way onto the careful clothing of passersby. And what they shouted.

Perhaps, he thought, this comparison to a motor was too much. Today was not a motor at all; today was, in fact, nothing at all which was inside him. Today was the river, not the street; the countryside, not the town. It was sleeping and not awake, like the big sawyers along the river of his childhood who cut hardwood for the town, how each woodcutter, after eating what was always a two-man lunch, could not move in the afternoon. Whatever was inside him, it was something that just stopped, as though a great horse or an elephant had simply sat, thereby saying *enough*.

SHE WOULD OF COURSE be waiting for him today, and he would of course be going. It was a match of two souls, if he could be so presumptuous, according to the universal law of magnets, and would not be denied. But somewhere in the night, what occurred to him was how much flesh, how many body parts, a soul can have. He dared not think such a thing, yet this was not the first time.

He had thought of her in terms other than words on many occasions now, and each one had weighed a little more. Until now he had become an elephant with it.

Today he would have to do something more, a remedy, an offering. More than words. With resolve he found an extra pair of legs in himself, and a ration of energy put away for emergencies. They got him to the door, and out.

His resolve was headstrong, that he would ask to stay the while of a second kiss, that he be allowed more than the small delicacies of sound, and the two-found dumb friends of the wild, her lips, her full lips.

Marriage, of course, he thought, though of course he could not say as much to her. But marriage is what he thought. Marriage as an avenue to her skin. A street paved to last, with sighs and with fingers, with lips more fully ranging. That place, he thought, for the heart but for the hands as well.

Perhaps he would tell her he was too thin a man after all these years, and that he needed the cure of exercise—and then a wink, something borrowed from the successful mannerisms of his brothers, who knew what was what, in these matters of the winking eye.

And perhaps she would understand his intimation, his wrestling with the words he could not say out loud to her.

He would ask this time for two kisses, and with it would assume the indulgence of everything meant in her granting him two kisses today, Tuesday. He made on himself the sign of the cross, pushed himself from the doorjambs the way one might push the frame of a small boat to give it motion, and went.

He felt as if he were apart from himself, risen from himself and pushing his own body out along onto the lake.

This was a different invisibility, stronger, with arms. It was what he had kept inside in maneuvering his walks on Tuesdays, not what he had been hiding from the outside world.

THEY HAD MET THIS way for so long because it would not have been proper to do otherwise. These matters are for family, and for arrangements. Nothing of the moment. In this way they were criminals. They were small in their crime, but only on paper. Nothing is bigger in a small town than two people in love without the permission of everybody.

It was that simple, and that absolute.

This explained the care they had taken with each other. It was the only explanation of how, after so many meetings, he felt as if he were climbing a trellis up to her, so much was the structure and mask they had made around themselves. To see her he had to pretend not to see her.

But that time had come to an end.

HE SAW THAT SHE saw him coming but did not see him, in that way they had pretended for so long.

But today the trick was no trick. In pretending not to see him, she was right: she did not see him. The trick was a trick on itself. The man coming toward her was not the man she knew. The man she knew was nowhere in sight, no matter what she saw, no matter what she pretended now.

He had been on all other days an invisible man, so discreet he seemed not even to move the air as he walked. On those days he was a small boat.

But today it was a different cloak he wore, a different face and a different air. He was undeniable. Something red and not gray walked in his place.

Though he was still at a distance, he saw that she could feel the air of his movement and the moment of his arrival touching her already.

Nothing in his demeanor, of course, was different. He was who he was in this town, after all.

But his eyes. Today they were not reconciled to the understood, to manners, to centuries, to the order of Nature and the nuances of the newspaper's last page. Today they were not eyes, not for seeing.

Today his eyes were mouths, for talking, and with them he told her as much. She could tell. Today as he approached, his eyes were speaking to her already, loud, with a summer-field voice. There was no whimper in them today, as she might sometimes have heard, that small dog she fed.

Nothing was mysterious in his eyes. They were big enough for her to be able to see things in them. She knew what they wanted, as if they themselves were the traditional intermediary between the two of them, between two hopeful bodies.

These eyes were no loose ends in his story, no leap ahead or to the side of the narrative: quite the opposite.

Today he had only one story. Here was no need of subplots or intrigue.

He simply wanted more than a kiss, more than his share, to share in fact no longer. Though he would not say it with words today, she knew because of his eyes. He wanted her hand, her hand and her lips, lips and all the everything more.

And yet that would be the joke, she would tell him later, because he had already gained entry into her.

SHE WAS RIGHT, HE would later say. He wanted more of her, and could not pretend otherwise.

He was coming to ask permission of her with his eyes for the two of them to come outside the world of souls a little. They were good together in the place of souls, good in love.

But today he wanted to say how he needed to rest a little in her body, as if he had gone in fact too far too fast, as if he had gone all the way through her, he would later tell her, all the way through her without stopping. And, therefore, without touching her.

And she would say, of course, she knew.

So his request today was to be for a little less of her. Some would say a little more, but she would understand.

To be sure, as she stood there, she seemed to take no offense in this, nor did she show any particular sadness. Enough was enough all around, she agreed with her eyes. The nodding of his head said souls had their places, as did the stars and fishing boats on the horizon.

But so did his hands have a place in hers.

She nodded her own head, and with that said to him she had no objection. And after so many years, his intentions she knew were, as the newspapers were bound to say, honorable. She rolled her eyes at him in the thought of just how honorable she knew him to be, and they both laughed.

However, no one else knew of their meetings, and so the townspeople would not be able to gauge their desire. It would seem to the town and on the back page as if this were almost an elopement, his making any inquiry concerning formal visits to her. Their romance, simply, would have to begin again. That is to say, it would have to begin differently.

He would come to see her the next time at the front door, and in front of everybody.

This is what he said to her now without words, this is what he intended. This is what he said to her with the mouths of his eyes, before he could get close enough to use breath: he was coming here today to tell her, here was the beginning of their story.